P9-BIM-767

LIES OF SILENCE

LIES OF SILENCE

BRIAN MOORE

LESTER
&ORPEN
DENNYS
PUBLISHERS

Copyright © 1990, by Brian Moore

All rights reserved. No part of this publication may be
reproduced in any manner whatsoever without written permission
from the Publisher, except by a reviewer who wishes to quote
brief passages for inclusion in a review.

FIRST EDITION

Published simultaneously by Lester & Orpen Dennys in Canada,
and by Bloomsbury Publishing Limited in the UK.

Canadian Cataloguing in Publication Data
Moore, Brian, 1921–
Lies of silence

ISBN 0-88619-275-7 (bound) ISBN 0-88619-322-2 (pbk.)

I. Title

PS8526.066L54   1990   C813'.54   C90-093271-6
PR9199.3.M617L54   1990

Printed and bound in the UK for

Lester & Orpen Dennys Limited
78 Sullivan Street
Toronto, Canada M5T 1C1

'My unconscious method is to find
the moment of crisis.' – Brian Moore

For Michael Dillon the moment comes just as he is making a decision
which he expects to bring him the greatest happiness he's ever known.
An ordinary man trying to get on with his life, he now finds himself
suddenly on the edge, faced with a moral choice which leaves him
absolutely nowhere to turn. The expectation of happiness is replaced
by a nightmare maze of dead ends.
Brian Moore's new novel addresses the starkest questions of right
and wrong, and the skeins of plot are tightened to a pitch of
suspense that leaves the reader breathless. To say that it is his best
yet is praise of a hyperbolic order, yet this is the culmination of
an extraordinarily fertile career. And it is, all too crucially, a book
for our times.

FOR JEAN

ONE

At a quarter to nine, just before going off work, Dillon went down to reception to check the staff roster for tomorrow. Two of the six women who came in to make breakfasts were reporting sick, so room service would be short staffed in the morning. He told Eileen, the clerk on the front desk, to ask Duffy to ring around and see if he could find replacements. But it would be a wasted exercise. He then went down the hall and had a word with Collis, the banquet manager.

'Bloody hell,' Collis said. 'I'm no help to you. Wouldn't you know it would happen on a day when we have two breakfast functions. And one of them's for eighty people.'

'Which one?'

Collis pointed to the appointments board:

ORANGE ORDER   CANADIAN LODGES
COMMEMORATION BREAKFAST
Speaker: Rev. Alun Pottinger   8.30 a.m. EMERALD ROOM
(Ticket Holders Only)

'Pottinger,' he said. 'I forgot.'

'Will there be special security?' Collis asked.

'I don't think so. He has his own minders. How many private luncheons do you have?'

'In the banqueting-rooms I have four. Full up. And the dining-room is fully booked.'

'Well, it's graduation week,' he said. He looked at the clock on Collis's desk. One minute past nine. She should be home now. He said good-night to Collis and made his last round of the day, stopping in at the lobby bar to sign a supplies list. The bar was the busiest part of the hotel and a favourite hangout for the university crowd. Last year he had changed the décor and hung large photographs of contemporary Irish poets and singers on the walls.

'Are you daft?' Mickey Cavan, the head barman, had asked him. 'Sure nobody will know who the half of these fellows are.'

'You may not,' he told Mickey, 'but most of your customers will.'

Tonight, the place was packed with celebrating students. He had to push his way through a jam of boys and girls, laughing, drinking, arguing. Last year Andrea was one of this crowd, her degree fresh in her hand, with no notion that he even existed. Fear came over him again. Don't think about it.

At the bar, there were four men serving. One of them, a temporary, saw him and went for Mickey. When Mickey brought the supplies list and put it in front of him, suddenly it was as though he had forgotten why he had come in here. Mickey was saying something, but the words were meaningless as the muted mouthings of the newsreader on the television set above the bar. He signed the supplies list without looking at it, said good-night to Mickey, and, in sudden panic, pushed his way out through the press of students. In the lobby he did not wait for the lift but ran up the winding staircase to his office on the mezzanine. He shut the door behind him and stood, feeling his heart thump. His office, lit by the yellow glow of a summer's evening, was still as a painting. He dialled her number. One of her flatmates answered.

'Just a minute. Hold on, please. Andrea? ANDREA?'

He would not ask her over the phone. He did not want to be told it over the phone.

'Hello?'

'It's me,' he said. 'Like to go for a walk?'

'It's after nine, Michael.'

'It will still be light for nearly an hour. Please?'

She hesitated. 'All right, I'll wait for you outside the house.'

At once, he was sure of the worst. They offered it and she said yes.

'Excuse me, sir.'

He looked up. It was Annie, one of the night cleaners. 'Can I do your office now, Mr Dillon? Are you off home?'

'Yes, go ahead.'

She came in, pushing her cleaning cart in front of her, stout, old, her legs encased in orthopaedic stockings. 'Safe home, then,' she said, as he went out.

His little red Renault was in its reserved parking space below the banqueting-room windows. As he went towards it, a taxi drove into the car-park and stopped. Two girls got out. They wore dance frocks and came towards the entrance to the ballroom. Hurrying, laughing, talking, they ran past without giving him a look. How old were they? Nineteen? He would be old to them.

'Come on, what's twelve years?' Andrea had said.

'A generation,' he said.

He got into the Renault and drove down towards the hotel security gates. A queue of cars was waiting to be admitted to the hotel grounds. Security was tight for the hotel had been bombed last year. The occupants of each car must get out and go into the adjoining security hut for a body search, while the car itself was checked over by the outside guards.

Gerry, one of the night men, saw his Renault coming and ran to open the exit gate. 'Good-night, Mr Dillon.'

''Night, Gerry.'

The gate shut behind him as he nosed the car out on to the Malone Road. Mountjoy Avenue, where Andrea shared an upstairs flat with two other girls, was less than five minutes away. As he drove up the Malone Road past rows of terraced Victorian houses, a police armoured car came towards him, lop-sided, like a damaged cardboard carton. It stopped at the cross street ahead. Five policemen climbed out of its rear, wearing combat jackets, their revolvers cowboy-low on their thighs. Wary, they crossed the street and entered a small grocery shop. Tonight, this familiar sight depressed him. Why should he stay, why should anyone in their senses stay here?

When he turned into Mountjoy Avenue he saw her waiting, wearing a loose blue denim shirt, jeans and scuffed loafers. She waved to him. As he drove closer, he tried to read an answer in her face and, when she got into the car, he leaned over and kissed her. She did not speak or look at him when his lips touched her cheek. 'Let's go on the towpath for a bit,' he said. 'Is that all right?'

She nodded. He put the car in gear and drove on. 'How are you?' he asked.

'Fine. Did you have a busy day?'

'How about *your* day? What happened?'

'I asked you first.'

So she did not want to talk about it. Maybe she didn't get it. But that, he knew, was wishful thinking.

'Well, it was pretty hectic,' he said. 'And tomorrow will be worse. It's graduation week at Queen's.'

'God, was it only last year – that tacky rented robe and you walk across the stage and they shake your hand and give you a scroll, and you think: Is this what I studied for, is this all it is?'

'I know.'

'Of course. I forgot. When was it *you* graduated?'

He did a small sad sum in his head. 'A long time ago.'

'Lunch at the Clarence,' she said. 'It's all part of the ritual, isn't it? I remember last year, we went there, three of us, right after the graduation ceremonies. We had it all planned, a table, a big celebratory lunch. But there was some mix-up in the reservations and we wound up eating sandwiches in the bar.'

'Pity you didn't know me then.'

'Just as well. If I'd met you before my finals, I wouldn't have passed them.'

She smiled as she said it. The first time he ever saw her was in the hotel. He had arranged conference rooms for an Arts Council symposium of Scottish and Irish poets. A BBC crew was covering the event and he noticed her at once, young, attractive, doing interviews with a sound and camera unit. Suddenly, she came up to him. 'You're one of the Irish poets, aren't you?' she asked, and in that moment all the wrong turnings he had taken in his life came back to sentence him.

'I was, once,' he said. 'Now, I'm a hotel manager.'

'Once a poet,' she said, and smiled at him. He noticed her accent.

'Are you American?'

'Canadian.' She kept looking at him. She was not smiling now. 'My name is Andrea Baxter,' she said. 'Would you like to have a drink when I've finished?'

That was it. She had started it. Tonight, she might end it, and now when he drove into the public car-park above the Lagan River towpath it came to him that if it were to end tonight, he had, inadvertently, chosen the perfect setting. For it was here, five months ago, that she had told him she loved him.

As they went down the narrow lane leading to the towpath, a courting couple came up, the boy's arm around the girl's waist, the girl's head on his shoulder. When Andrea saw them she moved ahead, single file, to let them pass undisturbed, going on alone down to the quiet of the river. Here, all was pastoral and still. Trees, heavy with leaves, creaked gently in the late evening breeze. In the river, lily pads floated on dark green currents. On the far bank, fields stretched to the horizon. Unlike most of the city's outskirts this place had not changed since those turn-of-the-century days when horses drew barges along this towpath, bringing loads of flax to the city's linen mills. Now, as then, it was a lover's lane, a place where couples went to be alone, lying hidden in the long grasses. He quickened his step and drew level with her. She stopped, looked down, and pointed at the current. 'See – a fish.'

He saw only green reeds rippling in the dark waters. 'Where?'

'Over there.'

'I don't see it.'

But, as he spoke, a silvery fish fluttered underwater like a falling kite. 'You can tell me,' he said. 'I'm expecting it.'

'Expecting what?'

'The meeting. What happened?'

She laughed. 'I was wondering when you'd ask.'

'Come on. What was it all about?'

'Well, it seems they're looking for someone to be head researcher for a new national arts programme. Apparently, Martin recommended me and Nigel Somerville wants to meet me next week in London.'

'For an interview?'

'Not exactly. Martin thinks I've got the job, if I want it.'

'But of course you want it.'

She turned to him. 'How do you know what I want?'

There were tears in her eyes. 'I mean, what were the last five months about, Michael? Just a romp in the hay, is that it?'

'Don't be ridiculous. I love you.'

'You love me but you'd let me go away?'

'What do *you* want?' he said. 'That's what matters.'

'I don't know what I want. I told them I wasn't sure – that I wanted to think about it. Shit, of course I don't want to stay here for ever. But is this job more important than you? What is it with us?'

'Listen,' he said. Suddenly, he knew what he must say. 'You've got to take the job. Because we're going to live in London, you and I.'

Did she believe him? Would he believe him, if he were her?

'Listen,' he said again. He had not planned any of this but now the half-formed wishes that had come to him night after night as he lay awake filled his mouth in an urgent rush of words. 'I'm going to tell Moira. And I'll speak to Eamonn McKenna, my solicitor, about getting a divorce. I want you to go in there tomorrow and tell them you're going to London to see Somerville. You can still do that, can't you?'

'Yes,' she said, 'but listen, Michael – '

'No, you listen. If you go to London next week I'll come with you. Keogh's in London, he's the Yank in charge of all of our hotels in Europe. He's the one who asked me to come back here and manage the Clarence. I've done a good job and they know it. I'm sure he'll fix me up with something in London. It won't be a manager's job, of course.'

'But if you're doing such a good job here they won't want you to leave.'

'I don't care. If he says no, I'll come to London anyway. I'll find something.'

She looked at him, then turned towards the dark currents of the river. It was as though he were no longer there. Suddenly, everything he had just said seemed foolish and impossible. They had never really talked about a future together. His thoughts of leaving Moira had been half-formed desires, not plans for action. He did not really know Andrea. She had come to Northern Ireland four years ago because her father, a Canadian engineer, had accepted a two-year contract with Short's, the aircraft people. When her parents returned to Canada she stayed on to finish her arts degree. There had been a boyfriend but Dillon did not know his name. She said she liked the Irish much better than the English 'because they're more fun'. But what was it she saw in him? He did not smoke pot or like rock concerts as she did. He was not knowing in bed as she was. He was married and hiding their affair from his wife. His job must seem boring

7

to her. He was a failed poet in a business suit. And yet he believed – although he could not explain why – that she loved him. From the moment she had said it to him, here on the towpath, they had seen each other almost every day. Often they would meet for an hour and in a rush of desire go to the hotel, get a key, and make love in an unbooked room. Yet he did not think of this as an affair. He had never been unfaithful before. He was filled with the excitement of being in love and sick with the fear of losing her. He knew that girls her age got crushes on married men. And got over it.

She turned back from the dark currents of the river. 'Is that what you really want, Michael?'

'Yes.'

'You're sure? Don't say it unless you're sure.'

'I'm sure.'

'All right, then,' she said, and kissed him.

Black became white. By voicing his daydreams he had made them real. 'I love you,' he said.

She took his hand and they walked on. 'What about Moira? Will she stay on, if you leave?'

'I think so. She's never been happy anywhere else.'

'What will she do?'

'I don't know. Maybe settle in full time, selling that jewellery and junk stuff.'

'Could she make a living at it?'

'I don't know.'

They rounded a bend in the river and saw a red sky ahead. On the horizon long veils of black smoke drifted towards them.

'Is that in the city?' she asked.

'No, it's in the other direction. Out by Lisburn.'

'Is it a fire, do you think?'

'It's probably deliberate,' he said. 'Farmers burning stubble.'

'It's late. Maybe we should go back.'

'Wait. Let's sit a minute. Please?'

To their left, he saw a break in the hedge. They went through it into a field of long grass. He tested the ground for dampness before they sat down, then lay back, looking up at the red sky. 'I can't wait to get away. Bloody place. I never wanted to come back here.'

'No kidding.'

They laughed, together. 'Yes, I believe I've mentioned that before.'

'Like a thousand times.'

He turned to her, meaning to kiss her. At once she pulled him down, kissing him in a fever as though they would begin to make love. But when he slid his hand along her thigh she held it in a restraining grip. 'You're sure about this, Michael?'

'Of course I'm sure. It's the best thing that ever happened to me.'

She released him and lay back in the grass. 'When will you tell her?'

'Tomorrow.'

'And then?'

'I'll move out. I'll take a room in the hotel until you and I go to London.'

'What if they tell you you have to stay here?'

'I told you. I'll go anyway.'

She sat up again, hands locked around her knees. 'I'm scared. Aren't you?'

'No. I'm happy.'

'Well, if you're happy . . . ' She turned to look at him. 'I wish it were over. I mean, I wish we were in London right now. You won't back out, will you? I mean, if you do, I wouldn't blame you. I'm not married. It's different for me.'

He reached up and caught hold of her, felt her body, tense, almost trembling. 'Listen,' he said. 'Do you realise that after tonight we can be together all the time? Tomorrow, when I move into the hotel, you can join me.'

'Yes, I could, couldn't I?'

He felt her body relax. She kissed him, then stood up,

brushing burrs from her jeans. She turned to look down at him, then stretched out her hand, pulling him to his feet.

As they walked back up the lane which led to the car-park, several couples were coming down, courting the coming darkness. In the car-park there were now twice as many cars as before. When he unlocked the door of his own car it came to him that this was the end of secret meetings, of lying in long grasses, sitting in parked cars, making love in empty hotel rooms. And an end to his evenings with Moira, waiting for her to go up to bed or take her shower so that he could slip out and make his nightly phone call. And, as though to remind him of those frustrations, when they drove back to Mountjoy Avenue all the lights were on upstairs in the house, which meant her flatmates were at home. So they sat in the car and he kissed her again.

'When will we meet tomorrow?' she said.

'Can you be at the hotel at seven?'

'OK.'

'We could have dinner together. A celebration.'

'It won't be a celebration, Michael. Not for you. I remember when I broke up with my boyfriend. I was happy I'd done it, but ...'

'Who was that boyfriend?' he said. 'Maybe now you can tell me?'

She laughed. 'Past history. Doesn't matter.'

She kissed him. 'Do you know what I'm worrying about? What if she won't let you go? I wouldn't.'

He laughed. 'I'll see you in the lobby of the Clarence at seven.'

'At seven.' She got out of the car and ran up to her front door. He watched her unlock the door, hoping she would turn and wave to him. He waited. She turned, waved, and went in.

As he drove home, a late northern summer's light cloaked the city's Victorian monuments and buildings in a ghostly, golden glow. Shopping areas were deserted. For years, people had been unwilling to walk the streets at night. He turned up towards

Millfield, driving through those parts of Belfast which had become the image of the city to the outside world: graffiti-fouled barricaded slums where the city's Protestant and Catholic poor confronted each other, year in and year out, in a stasis of hatred, fear and mistrust.

'But it was the Germans who destroyed Belfast,' his father used to say. 'It wasn't these Troubles, it was the bombing during the last war. After the war they cleared the bombsites, but they never rebuilt.' It was true, he supposed, for he had seen photographs of the pre-war city, orderly, ugly, Victorian. But what the war had begun, a quarter of a century of civil strife had worsened, so that now, beneath the new motorways which crossed the city like slash marks on a map, the old heart of Belfast, those thousands of small dwellings which housed people whose highest ambition was a job in a shipyard or a mill, lay in a continuing plague of poverty, decaying, without hope.

His house was in the north end of Belfast, part of that much larger city which surrounded the central ghettos, a quiet, unpublicised, middle-class Belfast where Protestants and Catholics lived side by side, joined by class, by economic ties, even by intermarriage, in a way the poor could never be. The house, unlike the others in their avenue, was rented, for Moira had said, 'What I really want is to buy a nice place on the other side of town, near your work.' When he told her that he had no intention of staying on in Belfast she ignored it.

The first time he met her – it was at a party given by mutual friends in London – she said, 'Do you like it here? I hate it. You could live six months anywhere in London and you'll be lucky if you know the name of the people next door. I can't wait to go home.'

'So you're going home?' he asked. Although he had known her less than five minutes he felt an ebb of disappointment. She was tall, beautiful, and very flirtatious. Already, he had thought of asking her for a date.

'I wish I could,' she said. 'I came here because I couldn't find a job at home. This girl, Clodagh Burke, she's a friend of mine, we were at UCD together – '

'You were at UCD?'

She laughed. 'You sound surprised. Well, as I was saying, Clodagh's started a little nursery school here in Hampstead and she asked me to come over and help her run it. If she makes a go of it, she wants to open a second school in Belfast. And I'll run it.'

'So you'll be going back eventually?'

'Maybe. Between ourselves, I'm fed up with teaching kids. I don't know what I want to do now. I'd love to go home but, for the time being, I'm stuck here.'

'It's ironic,' he said. 'I'm the opposite.'

'Why's that?'

'This American hotel group I'm working for has just bought the Clarence Hotel. They want me to manage it for them. And it's the last thing I want.'

'So what are you going to do?'

'I'm going. If I go to Belfast now and make a go of it, they've promised they'll bring me back to London and put me in charge of one of their hotels here. Which is what I *do* want.'

'So when are you leaving?'

'October.'

'I envy you,' she said.

Was that why, when two months later he asked her to marry him, she said yes? A few weeks ago in a drawer he found an old, discarded wallet. Inside was a colour photograph of a girl, tall, slender, smiling, wearing a low-necked dress, hair tumbled about her shoulders, a photograph a man might keep in his wallet to show to other men for the pleasure of knowing they envied him.

And, of course, they envied him. Was it only last year that

her habit of flirting with strangers still filled him with jealous rage? Beginning with his father who, tipsy at the end of the wedding reception, clasped Moira to him in a far from fatherly embrace, giving her a large, wet, lascivious kiss.

Now, as he drove up the Antrim Road, he thought of his father. Moira would, of course, telephone his parents at once. He could imagine his father listening to the news in his office in the back hall of Kinsallagh House Hotel, putting down the phone, rising to go and close the green baize door so that the kitchen staff would not overhear, then ringing him up.

'Michael, what's this I hear? I've just been talking to Moira. Have you thought of what this will do to your mother, have you? Never mind the damage to your career. Do you think you can walk off the job of running an important hotel and expect anyone in this business ever to take you seriously again? I might remind you this reflects on me. I recommended you to those people. I trained you – well, all right, early training here at Kinsallagh. And the Yanks, how do you think they're going to react? I can see Mr Keogh's face when you tell him you've walked off an important post just because you've met some little tart. Damn it, Michael, there are more important things in life than a piece of crumpet.'

At which point he would probably hang up on his father. But that would not be the end of it. His father, sole proprietor of Kinsallagh House Hotel, County Antrim, 'a fine old Irish country house, a listed building set in five acres of landscaped gardens, with magnificent fishing in the nearby Kinsallagh River', his father who had managed to live his life in a fantasy world, believing that his guests saw him as a landed gentleman who ran Kinsallagh House not as a hotel, but as a hobby, his father who could conveniently ignore the fact that to make ends meet he, the landed gent, must act as head waiter in the dining-room, and take orders for wine and drinks each evening before dinner was served, his father who had introduced him to the hotel business, who had been so impressed by his appointment to run the Clarence, 'A plum, Michael, once the finest hotel in the city. And it will be again, thanks to you.' To his father this would seem a personal insult, a family betrayal.

Ahead, as he drove into Winchester Avenue, the sky turned dark. He turned up the narrow entryway behind his house and parked the car in its usual place outside the gate of his back garden. There was no wind tonight. The garden seemed oddly still. He looked up at the house, half hidden by untended shrubs and hedgerows. There were no lights on upstairs. So, she was not yet in bed. He opened the gate and stood in the garden, waiting for the cat. But the cat did not come. Where was it? No matter how late he came home the cat would glide up swiftly, rub against his trouser-leg and mew for its food. It was an outside cat. Moira would not allow it in the house.

'Teddy?' he called softly. 'Teddy?' He waited, then shut the gate behind him and went up the garden path to the back door. Who would feed it when he was gone? He opened the back door, which was unlocked, and saw the false colours of television spill into the shadows of the back hall.

'Michael, is that you?'

He went into the sitting-room. She was not alone. 'We were just watching the end of *The Twilight Zone*,' she said, rising to switch the set off.

He turned to Peg Wilton. 'Hello, there.'

'Hello, Michael. Goodness, it's half ten. I had no idea it was so late. It was light until a minute ago.'

'The twilight zone,' he said.

Peg Wilton laughed, heaving herself up from the sofa, presented her large rump to him as she bent down to scoop several small objects off the coffee table. 'I'll leave these two pieces of jet, will I?' she said to Moira. 'And the tortoiseshell combs, is that right?'

'I'm not sure about the jet – oh, leave them, anyway,' Moira said. 'But I definitely have a customer for the combs. And, listen, Michael will run you home.'

'No, no.'

'It's no bother,' he said.

Peg Wilton smiled at Moira. 'As always, the gentleman.'

Was she being sarcastic? He knew she did not like him and, normally, would have been irritated at having to chauffeur her half a mile down the road. But tonight, in the same room with Moira, knowing that tomorrow she would have to be told, he wanted to escape. 'Listen, don't bother to wait up for me,' he said. 'Why don't you go on up to bed? I have some things to do.'

Moira ignored this. 'Come on, Peg, we'll go out the back. The car's in the entry.'

When they all three stepped into the garden he peered around in the darkness. 'Have you seen the cat tonight?'

Moira was not interested in the cat. She embraced Peg Wilton. 'All right, Peg, I'll give you a ring tomorrow. Around ten, OK?'

He went ahead of Peg and, opening the car door, pushed the front passenger seat back as far as it would go. Peg was a large lump of a woman. When he switched on the headlights, suddenly, ahead, he saw the yellow gleam of a cat's eyes. But this cat was a Persian. It ran in front of the car and jumped into a bush.

They drove out into Winchester Avenue. Peg said, 'I suppose these are busy days for you at the hotel?'

'Yes, it's graduation week.'

'Of course. And everybody goes to the Clarence afterwards. Especially now. It's marvellous, the change in that place since you've had the running of it.'

He stared at the road ahead. Who will take over the running of it now? They'll have to send someone from London. Again he felt a rush of happiness so strong that, unconsciously, he put his foot down hard on the accelerator, sending the car surging forward.

'Hold on, hold on,' Peg said. 'We're nearly here. The fourth door, the red one. There.'

He pulled in where she indicated and shut off the ignition. As he did, she leaned towards him and put her plump, ringed hand on his sleeve. 'Could I ask you something?'

'Yes, what?'

'You won't be annoyed with me, will you?'

'Why would I be annoyed?'

'Well, the thing is, Michael, I've decided to open up a place in Dublin. I've found a marvellous set of premises just off Grafton Street. The thing is, you see, I'll have to go up there to get it going. And that means I need someone to run my place here, someone with flair. And, to be frank, the person who would be ideal is Moira.'

Had Moira put her up to this latest lunacy? Running a bloody shop. But now, what did it matter? It might even help. 'What does Moira feel about it?' he asked.

'Well, that's the thing, you see. She thinks you've got some sort of prejudice about her working in a shop.' She smiled at him, the smile of an enemy. 'Is that true?'

'It's true,' he said. 'With her education, I think it's a waste.'

'But the thing is, as you know yourself, Moira isn't interested in teaching. I think this would be great for her. It would get her out. Meeting people. I think she'd love it.'

'Well, it's up to her,' he said, and at once felt Peg's fingers tighten on his arm.

'Do you mean it?' she said, and this time her smile was real.

'Of course.'

'Oh, good. Oh, I am pleased. Can I tell her it's all right, then? Or do you want to speak to her first?'

'No, you tell her,' he said. 'Tell her tomorrow.' For by this time tomorrow Moira would not be asking his permission about anything.

'But it will be all right, will it?'

'Absolutely.'

'Well, then, I'll run on in.' She pushed open the door of the little car. 'Thanks awfully, Michael. And thanks for the lift.'

'I'll see you to the door.'

'No, no, I'll be all right.'

As he watched Peg Wilton go to her door and open it, he remembered Andrea running up to her front door, turning, waving to him. Tonight my life has changed. Everything has changed. Everything.

He drove back down the Antrim Road and re-parked in the entryway. The light was now on in their bedroom window. Perhaps he could stay downstairs until she went to sleep? These last months he had found it easy to deceive her. She was the enemy of his freedom. But now he was sure he could not conceal his new happiness from her even for one night. Now she was no longer his enemy. She was his victim.

As he went up the garden path he heard a clattering sound behind him. The gate which he had not closed properly was swinging to and fro, hitting against the gatepost. He went back and in the light shining down from the upper window noticed something sticking out of the hedge behind the gatepost. A woman's handbag? But as he bent to retrieve it he saw that it was not a handbag. Teddy. He touched the body, hard and cold beneath its fur. The left side of Teddy's head was matted with blood, the jaw crushed as though it had been hit by a car.

Had someone, driving up the entryway, hit Teddy then thrown him over the hedge? Anyone using the entryway would most likely be a resident, might even know that Teddy was his cat. Sick, he lifted the small body and hid it carefully under a fuchsia bush. Better not to tell her tonight. He would bury it in the morning. Not that she cared about Teddy but a thing like this could set her off, making her ring up the police, accusing the neighbours, God knows what.

The back door was unlocked. He locked it now when he went

in. The phone began to ring and he hurried up the back hall to the hallstand where the receiver sat beneath a pile of coats. But, as he reached it on the third ring, the ringing stopped. She had picked up in the bedroom. Usually a call at this time of night meant an emergency at the hotel. So he lifted the receiver and heard Peg say, 'Remember, don't say anything. Be surprised.' Then Moira, hurriedly. 'All right. I think he just came in. Bye.'

As he started up the stairs her voice called down. 'Is that you?' He did not answer. At the head of the stairs he saw her figure, a black daguerreotype silhouetted against the light from the bedroom behind her. 'Did you pick up the phone?' her voice asked.

'Yes. What did Peg want?'

'Oh, it was just something she forgot to tell me about a piece of marquetry she bought.'

She turned and went back into the bedroom, sitting at her triptych mirror to begin the nightly brushing of her hair. As she picked up the brush she leaned forward and angrily plucked out a long strand, bright as a silver wire, examining it as though it were infected. Her blue cotton nightgown was cut in a deep V, exposing her long white back, the vertebrae like knuckles down her spine. She took up the brush again and began to comb her hair forward over her face with a jerking movement which brought back to him the sight of her kneeling at the toilet bowl, her finger in her mouth, retching as she vomited up half a box of chocolates or part of a cream cake, eaten less than an hour before.

Not that she had bothered to conceal her illness from him, once he discovered it. 'It's something that happens to me,' she said. 'It's called bulimia and there's nothing I can do about it. I suppose I should have told you before we got married. Yes, of course I should. Anyway, I don't want you telling people, now. Do you hear me, Michael? I mean it.'

But, of course, he had not heeded her. 'It's a form of anorexia,'

Sean Mullen, a gynaecologist, told him. 'They're women who want perfect figures and have a morbid fear of getting fat. They go on eating binges, sweets mostly, and vomit the stuff up. The theory is they want to become a stereotype of helpless, dependent female beauty. Is it someone you know?'

'Yes. But that stuff about wanting to be helpless and dependent doesn't sound right.'

'Are you sure?' Mullen said. 'These things don't always show on the surface. Whoever it is, she should think about treatment. Bulimics can be suicidal.'

Now, she tossed her head back, her hair swirling around like a ponytail as she caught sight of him standing behind her. 'What's the matter with you?' she asked crossly.

'Nothing.'

'Are you coming to bed?'

'In a minute. I have some bills to pay. Don't wait up for me.'

She turned again to her mirror, examining her face in a nervous, questing way, touching her cheeks, pulling the skin tight about her eyes, smoothing away imagined wrinkles. At thirty-three, she was as beautiful as ever, but in the past year she had begun to believe she was losing her looks. It was true that in her present, anxious, depressed state she no longer employed the flirtatious manner which men warmed to, but she was, indisputably, someone they turned to stare at in the street. Guiltily, he told himself that she would have no trouble finding a second husband. Whether she would want one was another matter.

'Good-night, then,' he said. She glanced at him through the mirror, but did not answer. He went out on the landing and into the small front bedroom which he had converted into a study. Here, arranged floor to ceiling in home-made bookshelves of bricks and plywood, were his books, most dating from his student days, some going back to his boyhood in Kinsallagh House Hotel – *his* books, Chekhov, Joyce, Eliot, Stevens, Yeats, Flann O'Brien, Lowell, Proust, Laforgue, Auden, Waugh, Greene,

Sartre, Tolstoy, a mix of novels, poetry, biographies – books he had jealously kept apart from those in the 'library' at Kinsallagh, those detective stories, spy novels and romances left behind by departing guests and used by his father to fill the bookshelves. *His* books: his passport to that other world he had once dreamed of joining. But tonight, looking at them, for the first time he thought of leaving them behind. Still, if he did not take them Moira might think that he had not really left home.

Outside, in the night silence, he heard the noise of a car coming up the avenue. It seemed to stop outside his house. He went to the study window and looked down. A white Ford Escort had parked across the street. The driver turned the headlights off and Dillon saw that there was a girl sitting beside him. The driver put his arm around the girl as if to kiss her, but did not. They sat frozen in that position for a long moment and then, as though aware she was being watched, the girl turned her head around and looked up at the house. At once, embarrassed, Dillon stepped back from the window. Behind him the light went off in their bedroom.

He sat down at his desk. He opened drawers, searching for the things he must take with him tomorrow. He collected his passport, his diploma from the *Ecole National d'Administration des Hôtels* in Lausanne, and his chequebook. In a second drawer he found copies of poems he had published in little magazines in his student days and some articles he had written for *Omega*, the student magazine he had helped to found. In the bottom left-hand drawer was a photograph album. He opened it. Pictures of his wedding day. The reception had been held in Kinsallagh House and there, on the front lawn, looking pleased with himself in rented morning clothes, was his father, armlinked with his mother who wore a large garden-party hat. The second photograph was of Moira's parents, Joe, the butcher, ill-at-ease in a badly fitting blue suit and Maeve, her mother, enormous in flowered chiffon. On the next page of the album was a photograph of Moira, alone in white satin, holding a bouquet of yellow roses, radiant, smiling, and somehow infinitely touching, like a tall twelve year old dressed up as a bride. The next page was blank. He shut the wedding portfolio and in that moment heard her call to him from the bedroom. 'Will you be long?'

'Probably. Go to sleep.'

'Shut your door, then. There's a light shining in my eyes.'

He did not shut the door. Instead, he reached up and switched off the desk lamp, leaving the study lit only by the reflected light from the street outside.

What will happen to her? She'll run Peg Wilton's shop for a while, but that won't last. With her, nothing lasts, jobs, friends, lovers, marriage, nothing. She wants to be loved. If only I'd been able to love her, to love *her*, not just her looks. But who really loves her? Her father, perhaps, but he thinks she's ungrateful. And her mother is afraid of her. Who does *she* love, Moira? No one, I suppose, least of all herself. She says she loves 'the crack here', the way people talk. 'Sure, there's no place like the North. I couldn't live anywhere else.' Yet, even here, she has no real friends.

In the street below, a car door slammed. He heard footsteps, loud in the night silence. He stood up and again looked out of the window. The white Ford was still parked opposite, but its occupants, the man and the girl, were strolling along, arm-in-arm, on his side of the street. When they drew level with his house, they stopped and embraced. As they did, he saw the girl move her head to the side, not kissing the man but instead looking up in his direction. Again he drew back, not wanting to be seen. He heard them walk on, then saw them cross the street and get into their car. The car engine started up. The white Ford drove slowly down the avenue and out on to the Antrim Road.

'Michael, what are you doing, sitting in there in the dark?'

'Nothing.'

'Come to bed, then.'

'Coming.'

When he went into the bedroom Moira switched on the bed light and looked at him. 'What's the matter with you?'

'Nothing. I was thinking.'

As he began to undress she turned to face the wall. When he lifted the sheet to get into bed beside her, she swivelled around and looked at him. 'What *were* you thinking? You've something you want to tell me, haven't you?'

He stared at her, tense. Her face, stripped of its make-up, looked naked, her untouched eyes seemed smaller than usual. How did she find out, how could she know, when I only decided tonight?

'Tell you what?' he said.

'Who do you think you are, Michael? What makes you believe I have to ask your permission about anything? Just go to hell!'

'What are you talking about?'

'I don't know why Peg bothered to speak to you, I didn't ask her to, it's none of your bloody business what I do, all this rubbish about me not working in a shop. I'll work wherever it suits me, do you hear me? I'm not stuffed full of middle-class snobberies, the way you are.'

'You mean Peg's shop?' he said. (Oh, God, is that all it is?) 'Listen,' he said. 'I wasn't against it, she must have told you that. Do what you want, if it makes you happy.'

'Do what I want? Thanks very much. What makes you think I need your permission to do anything?' She was sitting up in bed now, her long legs crossed in a Yoga position, ready for one of those meaningless fights that could go on for hours. 'I don't know what I'm doing here,' she said. 'Honest to God, I don't. I'm no use to you, you don't even like me any more –'

'That's not true.'

'It is true and you know it. I don't know why you married me, it certainly wasn't because you loved me. I know, I know, you liked the look of me, but you don't any more, do you?'

'Now, stop that,' he said.

'Stop what? What are you talking about? Nothing I do suits

you – you hate me, you hate this house, you hate being here, you hate your own country. I know you'd be far happier off in France or somewhere, anywhere but here – '

'I don't hate you,' he said.

'Listen, I don't blame you – look at me, what's happened to me?' She covered her face in her hands. She began to weep.

'Please,' he said. 'I've told you over and over, you're one of the most beautiful girls I've ever seen. It's not your looks, that's stupid!'

'Stupid. Oh, yes. All right, I know you think I'm stupid. I don't know who you thought you were marrying, maybe Maud Gonne McBride, or Simone de Beauvoir – how would that suit you? You could talk about poetry to your heart's content.'

'Stop it.'

'Stop what? It's the truth, isn't it? You're bored with me, you married me because you fancied me and now I've lost my looks you couldn't care less about me. The perfect proof is you used to make a fuss about my working in a shop but now, suddenly, you don't give a damn.'

'Maybe I was wrong about it,' he said. 'You know I have a prejudice about working in shops; remember I told you about me having to work in the gift shop at Kinsallagh when I was a kid – '

'Oh, yes, the young poet, too stuck up to sell a few Aran sweaters and souvenirs, yes, I remember, thanks very much, but I'm not you, I'm not stuck up like you – '

'Please?' he said. 'Moira, please, let's stop this.'

She rocked back on her heels and stared up at the ceiling, tears puddling her eyes. 'Why don't you leave me?' she said. 'You want to, don't you?'

He could not say it, not now, not with her weeping like this. 'Let's go to sleep,' he said. 'We'll talk about it in the morning.'

She caught her breath in a half-gasp. 'Talk about *what* in the morning?'

23

'Nothing. Come on. Put the light out.'

'Talk about *what* in the morning? About leaving me? That's what you said, isn't it?'

'I didn't say any such thing. I have a big day tomorrow. I want to go to sleep.'

Slowly, almost absent-mindedly, she wiped away her tears. She stared at him for a long moment, her face immobile as a mask, then lay down and turned to the wall.

'Do you want the sheet over you?'

She shook her head. He got into bed, careful not to touch her. He reached up and switched the bed light off. Here at the back of the house there were no street lamps outside. Darkness made strange shapes of the dressing-table and the bedside chair. Does she know? How could she? She doesn't even know that Andrea exists. No, it's nothing new, she's talked about me leaving her before. He stared at the night sky. Out there in the garden the cat lay dead. Perhaps it was better this way. She would not have fed him. He would have become a stray.

'Michael?'

'Mmm?'

'I won't go and work for Peg if you don't want me to.'

'I've told you,' he said. 'I was wrong. It's probably a good idea. Peg thinks you'll enjoy it.'

'No, listen,' she said. 'If I'm not wanted any more, I don't want to stay. I'll pack up and walk out of here tomorrow. There's lots of things I can do. I can go back to teaching. I mean, I'm not going to stay where I'm not wanted.'

Now was the time to say it. But if he did they would be up all night.

'Michael?'

'Mmm?'

'Don't leave me. Please?'

He felt his eyes burn as though he would weep. And then, what he dreaded happened. She moved across the bed and spooned into his back. 'Do you love me at all? Just a little bit?'

He turned and held her in an embrace. He kissed her, a traitor's kiss. 'Now, stop it,' he said. 'Let's go to sleep.'

TWO

But, of course, he did not sleep. He lay for hours beside her, listening to her breathing, feeling her body twitch slightly as her restless mind fled through the corridors of her dreams. When at last he dozed in a light, confused state, he was wakened suddenly by the noise of a car outside. He sat up, looked at her lying on her back, then got out of bed, intending to go to the bathroom. The dial on his bedside clock said four-fifteen.

As he passed the bedroom window, he looked out at the garden. A car had come into the entryway and was now parked in front of his own car. It was a white Ford. As he stood looking at it, the front door opened on the passenger side and the girl got out. She walked up to the back gate of his garden, unlatched it, and came inside. She stood, a shadowy figure, looking up at the house. He drew back from the window. He saw her turn to go out again. He heard the faint sound of the garden gate being closed. She got back into the car. The car door shut. The car headlights then blinked on and off. Were they signalling someone? It was the same car and the same couple who had parked at the front of the house, hours ago. Had they been watching the house all this time? A house in the Somerton Road was burgled last week.

He turned and looked at Moira's sleeping figure in the bed. She had not wakened. Now, coming up the entryway towards the white Ford, he saw the shadowy figures of two men. They went past the Ford and one of them quietly opened the garden gate. When he saw them come in, he turned and went quickly out on to the landing and down the stairs. He reached the ground floor, and stopped to listen. He heard a murmur of voices at the back door. He knew the back door was locked. At once, he turned and ran to the front hallstand where the phone was. As he did, there was a tinkle of broken glass behind him. He reached the hallstand but, in the darkness, fumbled among gloves and scarves, trying to locate the telephone receiver. As he picked it up, footsteps sounded behind him.

'Put that down,' a voice said. 'Stay where you are.'

A blinding light shone in his face. 'Where's the switch?' a second voice said. They were young voices, flat, male, Ulster accents. The blinding light came closer.

The hall light came on.

Facing him, a flashlight in one hand and a revolver in the other, was a hooded figure, its head masked in a woollen balaclava helmet, the eyeholes cut wide showing the cheekbones. The intruder wore woollen gloves, a cheap blue Western-style shirt with metal-clip buttons, faded jeans and running shoes. Behind him, standing by the light switch, was another, similarly dressed figure, also pointing a revolver.

He had seen them on the evening television news and in newspaper photographs, theatrical figures, firing revolver volleys over paramilitary graves, marching in parades with banners and flags. But like most people he kept well away from the events themselves so that now, for the first time in his life, he was looking at them, here in his house, real revolvers, faceless, staring eyes, scruffy boys in woollen masks. Who are they? Are they Protestants or Catholics – U D A or I R A? Is this one of those mistakes where they come in and shoot the wrong person?

'What do you want?' He heard the fear in his voice.

'IRA. Where's your wife?'

'She's upstairs, asleep.'

As he spoke, there was a sound of footsteps in the kitchen. Two more masked intruders came through the kitchen into the hall. One of them was very tall and carried a walkie-talkie. Both were armed. They went into the darkened sitting-room, then came out again. The tall one shut off his walkie-talkie, which had been making a crackling sound.

'Go up and bring her down,' the one with the flashlight told Dillon, then turned and pointed to the smallest member of the group. 'Volunteer, you go with him.'

The small one kept his revolver pointed at Dillon's back as they went upstairs. When they reached the landing, Dillon said to him, 'Wait here, would you? I don't want to frighten her.'

Blue eyes white-circled by the holes of the balaclava studied him for a moment. 'Is there a phone in there?'

'Yes.'

'Then I have to come in with you.'

Dillon switched on the landing light which permitted him to see into the bedroom. She was still asleep. He went into the bedroom and, as he did, she sat up.

'Oh!' she called in a half-shriek as though wakened from a frightening dream.

At once he ran to the bed and caught hold of her. 'It's all right, Moira, it's all right. It's me.'

'Oh, Christ,' she said. 'What are you doing up at this hour?'

Suddenly, the bedroom light came on. Standing by the switch was the small masked intruder, pointing his revolver at them. 'Ohh!' Moira gasped, but Dillon held her, pressing her tightly to him.

'Shsh! It's all right.'

She stared over his shoulder at the masked man, and then, surprisingly, eased herself out of Dillon's embrace. 'Who's he? What's he doing here?' she said in an aggrieved voice.

'Get up,' said the masked man.

'What do you want from us?' she said. She did not sound afraid.

'IRA. Put something on. We're goin' downstairs.' He turned to Dillon. 'You too. The pair of you, get dressed.'

Dillon hesitated, then went to the phone. At once, the small intruder ran towards him, pointing the gun. 'Wait,' Dillon said. 'The phone's on a jack.' He bent down, unplugged it, and offered it to the intruder who hesitated, then took it. 'Will you wait outside a moment?' Dillon asked. The intruder nodded and went out on to the landing.

Moira went to the chair where she had left her clothes and in a swift fluid movement pulled her nightgown up over her head and stood, naked, her slender body ivory-white under the ceiling fixture. At once Dillon turned to see if the masked youth was watching. But the gunman had his back to the door. Moira now put on underpants and the red shirtwaist dress she had worn last night. 'Where are my shoes?' she asked.

He found them at the foot of the bed. He saw her sit down at the dressing-table and take up her lipstick. 'Hurry,' he said.

She turned to him. 'What's the hurry? You're not dressed yourself.'

Hastily, he found jeans and a rollneck sweater in the wardrobe, put them on and slid his feet into loafers. As he did, she sat doing her eyes with an eyebrow pencil. In all the time he had known her she had never wanted to show herself to anyone without first putting on her make-up, and now she began to draw a line along the edge of her eyelid as though the gunman were a delivery boy who could be kept waiting. But, watching her, he saw that her hand was shaking. He went to her and, bending over her, said quietly, 'Look, it's some mistake. We'll be all right.'

As he spoke he heard voices outside. The first gunman, the one with the flashlight, came into the room. 'What's keepin' you?' the gunman asked in his high angry voice. 'Come on. Get downstairs.'

The smaller gunman then came in and, nudging them with his revolver, herded them out on to the landing. The hall light had been switched off again and the other gunman used his flashlight to guide them as they went down. 'Stay by the front door,' the one with the flashlight told the small one. Then, as if he were familiar with the layout of the house, he went into the dark sitting-room and pulled down the window blind. He turned on a small reading lamp and beckoned them to come in. 'Sit over there,' he said, pointing to the sofa which faced the television set. He shut the door, drew up a chair and sat down facing them.

'We're going to be here till the morning. There'll be somebody in here with you all the time. Don't try any tricks and you won't be hurt.'

There was something about this gunman, an electric tension which made him seem dangerous. As he sat in the chair his left leg jiggled in a nervous spasm. He blinked constantly, as though the light hurt his eyes which were red-rimmed, the eyelashes charred as though in a fire or an explosion. Behind the disguise of his paramilitary pullover and hooded menacing headmask, the high-pitched voice and slight adolescent body proclaimed that this was a child with a gun, excited as a child is when suddenly the game becomes dangerous.

Dillon looked at Moira. She sat upright on the sofa as if it were a hard-backed chair, her hands folded in her lap, her knees pressed together in a prim posture, as though she, not the gunman, were in charge. She stared at the hooded faceless face with a fixity of expression which seemed to aggravate the gunman's blinking eyes and jiggling left leg.

Now the only sound in the room was the tiny tremulous beat of the intruder's rubber-soled shoe on the worn carpet. As though unable to bear her continuing stare, the gunman shifted his position and said in his high flat Belfast voice, 'What are you lookin' at?'

Moira let the question drift for a moment. Then, spitting the words out, she said, 'Not much.'

Instinctively, Dillon moved across the sofa to prevent the gunman from hitting her. But the gunman sat totally still. His leg no longer jiggled. Then, behind the wool mask, he laughed. 'Cheeky, aren't ye?' he said. 'You stuck up wee bourgeois bitch.'

'You don't know what bourgeois means. You're too thick,' Moira said. Her accent had changed: she now spoke in the flat Belfast tones of the gunman himself. 'And, for your information,' she said, 'I was born and brought up in the Falls Road. So don't come that with me.'

'You're a long way from the Falls now, aren't ye?' the gunman said.

Moira shook her head, smiling an angry smile. 'No, I'm not,' she said. 'Nor never will be.'

The gunman's foot began to jiggle again. 'Whereabouts in the Falls?'

'Divis Street.'

'I suppose your da's a policeman,' the gunman said, his voice unhinged by anger.

'He's a butcher,' Moira said. 'Not that it's any of your business.'

The jiggling foot stopped. The gunman leaned forward in his chair, holding the revolver between his thighs, pointing it at Moira like some reptilian penis. Blinking his small eyes, he stared her up and down, from her sandalled feet to her long bare legs, her slender body, her pale face, her long, dark, tumbled hair. It was a stare so overtly sexual that Dillon, watching, stiffened and sat tense. The gunman, ignoring him, edged his chair a little closer to her. 'You're not helpin' yourself, you know,' he said to her. 'Are you lookin' for me to hit you?'

'Leave her alone!' Dillon said. He stood up. At once, the

31

gunman turned to him and shouted in a high angry voice, 'Sit down, you! Mind yourself! Sit down!'

The shout, loud in the quiet night, brought footsteps hurrying towards them. The door opened and the two gunmen Dillon had seen earlier came in at a rush, revolvers up. Three revolvers were now pointed at him. It was as though he faced a firing squad. 'What's up?' one of the newcomers said in an urgent whisper.

The high-pitched angry voice answered. 'It's all right. It's nothin'.'

A gun poked into Dillon's chest. 'Sit down, you.' He was pushed and sent sprawling on the sofa beside Moira. He looked up into the floating faceless eyes of the tall youth. 'What do you want with us?' he said. 'Are we hostages here, or what? And why is this bastard annoying my wife?'

'I wasn't annoyin' her, she was annoyin' me!' The high-pitched voice was almost a scream.

The tall gunman turned away from Dillon and said, 'Do you want to wake the whole street?' He beckoned to the other gunman who had come in with him. 'Mind them, will you?' Then, in a cold tone, 'Volunteer, will you step outside for a moment?'

He and the high-pitched one went out, closing the door behind them. The new guard, a fat boy, sat down in the chair vacated by his predecessor. Like the others he seemed to be a teenager. He put his revolver on a nearby table and, fumbling in his shirt pocket, produced a packet of cigarettes. He hesitated for a moment, then offered the cigarettes to Moira and Dillon. They shook their heads, whereupon he put the packet back in his pocket.

Dillon saw that Moira was trembling. He moved close to her. She turned to him, tears in her eyes. 'What do they want?' she asked in a whisper. He shrugged to say he did not know. He tried to put his arm around her, but she shook it off as though he had done something indecent in front of a stranger.

What *could* they want? He had read that sometimes they went into people's houses and held them hostage for a few hours while they borrowed their cars to carry out a bombing or a shooting. This was a well-off part of the city. There might be some High Court judge or Unionist politician living near here who they want to kill. Or a police barracks they're planning to bomb. 'We'll be here till the morning,' the high-pitched one had said.

He tried to count. There are four of them in the house. And the man and the girl, keeping watch outside in the white Ford. Did they kill Teddy? Could be. If he came up, mewing for his food, drawing attention to them? Was that it? It can't be us they're after. We are being used in some way.

He turned again to Moira. 'Listen,' he said in a low voice. 'It's not us they want. If we do what they tell us, we won't get hurt.'

'How do you know what they want?' Moira said in a loud hysterical voice. 'They're in our house, they're waving guns around, they're the same ones who kneecap kids and blow up innocent people instead of the ones they're trying to kill, and you say they won't hurt us. Well, they're going to hurt somebody, aren't they?'

When she said this, Dillon turned to look at the fat young guard who was listening, half nodding his head as though he agreed with her. When she finished, the guard leaned forward and spoke in a quiet, pleading, tone. 'Missus, I'm sorry, but, listen, what your husband says is right. We're not here to hurt you, but I'm just advisin' you, that other volunteer who was in here before me, *he* might hurt you, if you annoy him. I'm sayin' this for your own good. Your husband's right. Do as you're told and you won't get hurt.'

'But somebody's going to get hurt,' Moira said in a tremulous voice.

The fat guard did not answer.

They sat then, in silence. Dillon could hear people moving

about in the corridor outside. After a few moments, Moira began to weep, gasping, clenching her fists as though to stifle her tears. He put his arm around her and this time she did not shake him off.

She wept. He held her, wanting to comfort her. No matter what these people said, they could both be dead by morning. He did not believe in God, in religion, or in any order or meaning to this world. Once he had thought he was a poet, had hoped that his work would be read, that writing would be his purpose in life. It had not happened. He had believed that he loved Moira, but he was wrong. He had believed that, tonight of all nights, at last his luck had changed, that tomorrow he would have the courage to tell her the truth and go off to a new life, away from her. But how could he turn around tomorrow and tell her, after what had happened tonight? He looked at her now, weeping, angry, afraid of her captors, and felt, not love, but pity and despair. If only he had decided to leave her a month ago, none of this would be happening. The house would be empty, Moira would be living with her parents or someone like Peg. Once again, his life had taken a wrong turning. Once again, he had acted too late.

Footsteps. The door opened. The tall youth appeared in the doorway, his short-wave radio emitting a crackling noise. He pointed to Dillon. 'Where are your car keys?'

'In the bedroom. Upstairs.'

'Come on. Get them.'

He stood up and followed the tall youth out into the dark hallway. The flashlight guided him as they went upstairs. On the landing he switched on the bedroom light and went in. His car keys, change, and wallet were on the bedside table. A voice behind him said, 'Give them over.' He did as he was told. They went back downstairs, their footsteps creaking on the stairboards beneath the worn carpet. In the hall, the masked face turned towards him. 'How much petrol is in your car?'

'The tank's half full.'

'OK. Go on inside, now.'

When he opened the sitting-room door, Moira, hunched up on the sofa, turned and looked at him, anxious and relieved. Ashamed, he realised she had been frightened for him. 'Are you all right?'

He nodded. 'Shut the door behind you and sit down,' the fat guard told him. He heard the tall one go down the hall into the kitchen and, a moment later, the sound of the back door slamming.

They are going to use my car. They will drive it somewhere and before the night is over they will murder someone. Or they will put a bomb in it and leave it somewhere to blow up. Any minute now, they will drive away.

But they did not drive away. He listened but did not hear the car start up in the entryway outside. Minutes passed, Moira got up, walked from one end of the room to the other, then turned to the fat guard. 'I have to go to the bathroom.'

The guard nodded, then went to the door and called, 'Volunteer?'

Someone came from the kitchen, shining a flashlight in the dark hallway. When he came into the room, Dillon saw with dismay that it was the first IRA man, the angry one who had upset Moira.

'She has to go to the toilet,' the fat guard said.

The angry one nodded. 'Come on, then,' he said to her. 'Where is it? Upstairs?'

'Yes.'

Dillon stood. 'I'll go with you,' he told her.

'Sit down,' the angry one said. 'If you want to go, you'll go one at a time.'

Moira put her hand on Dillon's arm. 'I'll be all right,' she said. The angry one followed her out, shutting the door behind them.

Dillon listened, straining to catch every sound. He heard the creaking of the stairboards and the sound of a door shutting. A moment later the silence was broken by the noise of a car passing in front of the house. Was that his car? What's happening upstairs? He thought of the angry one's sexual stare when Moira started to bait him. She is alone with him, up there.

He stood. At once the fat guard raised his revolver. 'Listen,' he said to the guard. 'Couldn't we go up now, you and I? I don't trust that bastard.'

'You don't trust what?' the fat guard asked.

'You know what I mean,' Dillon said.

'Interfere with her?' The fat guard shook his head. 'No, no, not to worry. He wouldn't do that.'

'How do you know? I'm asking you a favour. Let's go up.'

'We don't fuck around with women when we're on an operation,' the fat one said indignantly. 'That's not on. Never. This is a military operation.'

'You're not a fucking army,' Dillon said in sudden rage. 'Military operation, don't make me laugh.'

'You watch yourself,' the fat guard said. 'Sit down. You mind what you say, do you hear me? That Volunteer that's upstairs with your wife, if you said that to him, he'd belt you in the mouth, so he would. Look, I don't want no trouble from you. Just take it easy. Your wife will be down in a minute.'

He looked at the clock. It was twenty-past five. He sat down again. Five minutes passed.

'Well, where is she?' Dillon burst out. The fat guard lowered his head as if pondering the question. The balaclava headgear, like some medieval helmet, gave him the look of an actor in costume for a Shakespearian play.

Then, from upstairs came the sound of someone hammering on a door. The medieval head jerked upright. A voice called out something Dillon did not catch. The fat guard got up, went to the door, and opened it. 'Kev?' he said nervously.

Again, there was a knocking sound. This time Dillon and the guard heard clearly the angry one's high-pitched voice. 'Do you hear me? Come out, or I'll break the door down.'

The fat guard turned to Dillon. 'We'd better go up. There's only me and him in the house. Come on.'

He gestured with his revolver and followed Dillon out into the front hall where he turned on the light as they went upstairs. The bathroom was on the first-floor landing. As they reached the landing, the angry one came towards them, his voice trembling with rage and anxiety. 'She's been in there far too long. And the last wee while she's been pullin' on the chain. She's coverin' up somethin'.'

Suddenly, Dillon thought of the bathroom window with its ten-foot drop to the roof of the garden shed below. He moved quickly past the gunmen and knocked on the door. 'Moira! Moira, it's me. Are you all right?' He put his ear to the door. Inside, he heard the cistern filling with water. A hand shoved him aside. Kev, the angry gunman, began to bang his shoulder against the door.

The noise alarmed the fat one who said, 'Shsh! You'll wake the whole street up. Wait.' The fat one took a wallet from the back pocket of his jeans, pulled out a plastic credit card and carefully inserted it in the door-jamb below the lock. Wiggling it up and down, he turned the door handle. The door opened. As it did, Dillon, heartsick, heard the sound of something falling on to the roof below.

The bathroom light was on. There was no one in there. The bathroom window was open. It was a small window, three feet high by three feet wide. The gunmen ran towards it. Kev reached it first, peered out, then hoisted himself up on the windows, stuck his revolver in his belt, swung his legs out and jumped into the night. They heard him crash on the roof of the shed below. Dillon ran to the window with the other guard, peering out. On the slanting roof of the shed, Moira was crawling down towards the gutter, preparing for the second drop to the garden path below. But Kev had scrambled up and now slithered recklessly towards her. As he did she turned, saw him, and screamed, 'Help! Help!' But, as her voice cried out, high and loud in the darkness, Kev was on top of her, his hand covering her face.

Dillon rushed out of the bathroom. He ran down the stairs, the fat guard behind him. 'Stop,' the guard called after him in a panicky voice. 'Do you want to get shot?'

He turned, looked back at the guard, then ran through the kitchen out into the garden.

Coming towards him, running footsteps. Two masked men had come in from the entryway, a flashlight swivelling crazily as they rushed towards the garden shed. Dillon ran in the same direction and, as he did, saw the men more clearly. One of them, the tall youth who had taken his car keys, shone his flashlight up to the roof. 'What happened?' he called in a low voice.

Above them outlined against the night sky was Kev, clutching Moira in front of him like a hostage, his hand over her mouth. 'It's OK,' Kev whispered. 'I have her.'

The fat guard had come up behind Dillon and now his revolver jammed against Dillon's spine. 'Stay where you are.'

'Moira?' Dillon called.

The tall gunman turned and punched him in the stomach. 'Shut up.'

Dillon, gasping from the pain of the blow, saw them help Moira down from the shed roof, the flashlight briefly lighting her red dress, her long bare legs. 'Put the light out,' the tall gunman said in an urgent whisper. 'Get the two of them inside.'

The light went out. In the darkness Dillon tried to go to Moira, but the fat guard kicked his shin. 'Get inside, you, or I'll fuckin' kill you.'

Pushed by the gunman, he stumbled towards the kitchen door. Ahead of him he saw Moira, her mouth still covered by Kev's hand. He heard frightened, angry voices.

'What the fuck were you doin'?'

'I was doin' nothin'. I had to let her go to the bog and she jumped out the window. She's a fuckin' nutter.'

Once they were all inside the kitchen, the tall one said, 'Get back in the room, the two of you.' He was speaking, not to Dillon and Moira, but to the fat guard and Kev. As he spoke, he switched on his short-wave radio. Then he and the other one went outside again.

As soon as they had gone, Kev turned on his flashlight, shining it on Moira's face. Taking her by the arm he shoved her through the kitchen into the hall. Dillon followed, the fat guard's revolver poking at his back. When they entered the sitting-room the lamp was still on and he saw that Moira's knees were skinned and bleeding from her fall. Her red dress was ripped at the shoulder, showing the thin white strap of her bra. Kev shut the door and pushed her viciously, sending her sprawling on to the sofa. Dillon started forward, grabbing Kev's arm. 'Leave her alone.'

Kev wrenched himself clear of Dillon's grip. 'What did you say?'

'I said leave her alone, Kev.'

Kev's red-rimmed eyes blinked as though he had been hit. He turned to the fat guard. 'What's he talkin' about?'

The fat one, suddenly uneasy, sat down, straddling a chair back to front. 'No idea.'

Kev turned back to Dillon. 'My name is not Kev. Who said my name is Kev?'

Dillon did not answer. Kev looked over at the fat guard who avoided his stare. Then, in his high hysterical voice, he said, 'There'll be no more talkin' here.' He pointed to Dillon. 'Sit down, you.'

'Let me go to the kitchen and get some Bandaids and clean those cuts,' Dillon said.

'I'm all right,' Moira said. 'Stay here, Michael.'

He sat down beside her and took her hand in his. There was a new tension in the room. It was as though by her attempt to escape Moira had altered the balance of fear. Now it was their captors who were afraid. Had anyone heard her scream for help?

Had a neighbour looked out and seen what was going on in the garden? Was someone, even now, telephoning the police?

As though confirming this thought, Kev suddenly said, 'Put the light out.' The fat guard switched the light off. Kev went to the window and pulled the blind halfway up. Across from the house the white Ford was parked. The street was deserted. Kev watched for a moment, then pulled the blind down again. The light went on.

Kev's hand reached up under the woollen mask to scratch his face. He stared agitatedly at the fat guard who pulled out his cigarettes and held them out, offering them to Kev. Kev hesitated, then took a cigarette. The fat guard struck a match and both lifted the bottom part of their masks so that they could put the cigarettes in their mouths. Dillon saw that Kev's chin was hairless as a child's. His cheek was red with painful acne sores. He and the fat one, puffing at their cigarettes, turned away from Dillon and Moira, as if to hide their faces. After a few puffs the fat one said uneasily, 'We should be keepin' dick.'

'Put them out, then,' Kev said hurriedly. Hastily, they stubbed the cigarettes out and put the butts in the pockets of their jeans. Kev began to walk up and down the room, waving his arms as if to dispel the smoke, then sat down, visibly agitated, and after a moment Dillon saw him turn away and begin to scratch his acne under the woollen mask. As he did, he winced as if in pain. Dillon, watching him, realised with a start that Kev, though hiding his face from Dillon and Moira, was facing the wall mirror above the bookcase. Dillon turned and looked at Moira, but Moira was lying back, staring at the ceiling as in a trance.

Again Dillon turned to look at Kev, and stiffened in shock. Kev, believing himself unseen, had raised his woollen mask and was scratching at a sore just under his left eye. In the mirror Dillon saw, at last, the face of an adolescent boy, pitted with acne, an almost feminine mouth with bow-shaped lips, a thin neck, a sharp pointed nose. He saw it only for as long as it would take to focus and press a camera shutter and then Kev pulled down the woollen mask once more and turned in his direction, unaware that he had been watched. He picked up his revolver. Once again his left foot began to jiggle in involuntary spasm.

'Stop that jiggin', will you?' the fat guard said suddenly. 'It's drivin' me nuts.'

'Fuck you,' Kev said, but put his hand on his thigh, suppressing the tremor. He stared over at Moira, his red-rimmed eyes intent as he eyed her body. She looked at the ceiling, ignoring him. 'What do you see up there?' he said to her, and laughed. 'You're a real nut case, aren't you?' He turned to the fat guard. 'Fancy us bein' landed with a nut case.'

'It's OK,' the fat one said. 'Nobody heard her.'

'How do you know?' Moira said.

Her words fell like a sentence on the room. They sat then, all four of them, listening for sounds. Dillon, who, in the insomniac nights of the last months had often been awake in these hours, knew that Belfast, at night, was quiet as a village in rural France. It was quiet now. No one heard her. No one will come.

Suddenly, in the corridor outside, a crackling noise and muffled voices on a two-way radio. Kev and the fat one exchanged anxious looks. Kev got up and again walked across the room, waving his arms to dispel the cigarette smoke.

'Open the window,' the fat one suggested.

Kev shook his head and returned to his seat. They heard footsteps in the hall. The door opened and the tall gunman entered. He looked first at Moira, then at the two guards. 'All clear,' he said. 'Take a break. I'll mind them.'

Kev and the fat one at once stood up and left the room. The tall youth pulled a chair towards them, straddling it, then hitching it closer so that he sat directly in front of Moira and Dillon.

'That was a stupid trick you just played,' he said to Moira. He turned to Dillon. 'If the pair of you don't co-operate with us tonight, you're goin' to be sorry. If not now, then later on – a week from now, a month from now. We won't forget you. If anybody asks you any questions about tonight, you know nothin'. Is that clear?'

Dillon did not answer.

'Because this isn't over, this operation, it's just beginning. I hear your wife was shootin' her mouth off, earlier on. I don't think she realises. Do you know what I mean?'

'Realises what?' Moira said suddenly.

He ignored this. He turned to Dillon.

'It's up to you to keep her in check, do you hear? For her own good.' He sniffed. 'Do you smoke?'

Dillon shook his head.

'Either of you?'

Again, Dillon shook his head. The tall youth at once stood up, went to the door, opened it, and called softly, 'Volunteer?'

After a moment, the fat guard appeared in the doorway.

'You were smokin' in here?'

'Just the one cigarette. Sorry, now.'

'Both of yous?'

Kev now loomed up in the doorway. 'You too?' the tall youth asked.

Kev nodded. 'Sorry, now.'

'Shit!' the tall youth said. 'What do you mean, sorry? Did you lift your mask?'

'They didn't see us,' the fat guard said. 'We were turned away. It was just a wee puff, just for a minute.'

The tall youth looked at them, then shut the door on them, leaving them outside. He came back and sat down again, facing Moira and Dillon. 'You people are Catholics, is that right?' he asked.

'None of your business,' Moira said.

'I mean, if you saw anything you shouldn't I don't think either of you would say anythin', would you? *Would you?* I'm not threatenin', mind. I know you probably don't have any more time for the Brits than the rest of us.'

'Do you, indeed?' Moira said. She turned and stared at him. At once Dillon took hold of her hand, squeezing it in warning. But she pulled free and turned again to the gunman. 'Who the hell do you think you are, telling us what to do? Do you know what I've been sitting here thinking? Whose fault is it that you're in my house tonight? It's my fault. I don't know how we let you get this far. If there was a vote tomorrow among the Catholics in Northern Ireland you wouldn't get five per cent of it. You're just a bunch of crooks, IRA or UDA, Protestants or Catholics, you're all in the same business. Racketeers, the bunch of you. There isn't a building site in this city or a pub that you or the UDA don't hold up for protection money. *Protection money!* Military operation, my foot! You've made this place into a bloody shambles and if it was handed over to your crowd tomorrow, lock, stock and barrel, you wouldn't have the first notion of what to do with it.'

'Shut your mouth,' the tall youth said. 'Do you hear me? Shut your mouth, or I'll shut it for you.'

'Go on, hit me, hit me,' Moira said.

'What's the use? You're just a woman, you don't know what you're talking about.'

'No? I'll tell you one thing I *do* know. You're not fighting for anybody's freedom. Not mine, not the people of Northern Ireland's, not anybody's. The only thing you're doing is making people hate each other worse than ever. Maybe that's what you want, isn't it? Because if the Catholics here stopped hating the Prods, where would the IRA be? And the worst of it is, I'm wasting my breath talking to you because you're too stupid to know the harm you've done.'

The faceless eyes in the woollen mask stared at her, unblinking. 'Have you finished?'

'Would you like more?' Moira said.

He stood up, went to the door, and opened it. 'Get in here, the both of you,' he said. Kev and the fat guard appeared from the hallway. 'And I want quiet. Dead quiet. No talkin'.'

He went out into the hall, shutting the door behind him. Kev and the fat one took their former seats. Kev looked at Dillon. 'Did you say we were smokin'?'

Dillon did not answer.

'The pair of you, you're goin' to be sorry you ever met me,' Kev said.

'Shsh.' The fat guard jerked his thumb at the door. Kev nodded, then stared at Moira, that hungry stare, lascivious, mixed with hatred. Dillon also looked at her. She sat there, angry, frightened, but brave as he was not. She was the one who had tried to escape, she was the one who stood up to them. She was the one they feared. He was the one they hoped to reason with. He thought back to what the tall one had said before her outburst. *This isn't over. This operation is just beginning.* Perhaps they were not just going to use the car? Perhaps they had something else in mind?

And then it came to him. They might be planning to blow up the hotel. Bombing hotels to frighten off tourists was one of their tactics. They would need his car to get the bomb past the security gates. With him driving it? And maybe Moira in the car as well?

At that moment the door opened and the tall youth came in, his radio crackling faintly. 'Put the light out,' he whispered. At once Kev jumped for the switch. The room went black. 'No torches, nothin',' the tall one's voice said. 'Mind them two. Dead quiet, dead quiet, do you hear?'

In the darkness the heavy coldness of a revolver pushed under Dillon's ear. Beside him, Moira gave a small gasp as though the same thing was happening to her. In the dark he could hear his captors' breathing. The radio static started up again. A girl's voice spoke. 'Unit two, unit two?'

'Unit two, come in,' the tall youth said.

'Police on foot comin' from the Antrim Road.'

'How many?'

'Four. They have radio. Radio silence, over.'

'Over.' The radio static ceased. The tall youth said, 'I'm goin' out the back.'

Dillon heard him go down the hall into the kitchen. The revolver barrel below his ear shifted slightly and the fat guard whispered, 'Mind yourself, now, mind yourself. Quiet.'

Then Kev, whispering to Moira, 'Quiet, you, or I'll blow your fuckin' head off.'

The shallow excited breathing of his captors, the touch of steel below his ear, the knowledge that policemen, armed, and, most likely, in radio contact with an armoured police car, were turning in from the Antrim Road and coming up the avenue towards the house, perhaps alerted by some neighbour who had heard Moira scream and seen the goings on in the back garden, these thoughts, these sensations, filled Dillon with a confusion of fear and hope. Somewhere out there the police are coming towards this house, watched by the man and the girl in the white Ford, and perhaps by other IRA, armed, ready to open fire. What if the police ring our doorbell? Will that start the shooting?

Suddenly, he was at one with his captors, trapped, waiting for violence to start, praying that the police would pass by. How often had he read of innocent bystanders, even children, being killed in these battles.

If Moira and I are killed now it will be for nothing. We will die and be part of that endless mindless chain of killings. The police will not save us. Let them go past. Let them go past.

In the silence he heard the door open behind him. Involuntarily, he turned, but the revolver barrel dug into his neck, forcing him to keep still. Someone had come into the room and was moving past him. Facing the window, as he was, he saw this someone pull the blind slightly askew, giving a partial view of the street. A voice whispered, 'Comin' up now. Four of them.'

They heard it then, coming up the avenue, the slow tentative sound of a police armoured car. At once, the tension in the room became acute. The sound was louder now and, suddenly,

45

in the chink of window, lit by the street lamp outside, Dillon saw four armed policemen walking on the far side of the avenue, moving warily, looking right and left, covering each other. They moved on out of sight and then the vehicle rumbled past, grey, menacing, blind, the snout of its machine gun circling like some strange proboscis. It moved on.

Seconds later, it stopped. A voice in the street called something. A second voice answered.

They're coming back, Dillon thought.

Then, the person at the window whispered, 'It's OK. They're pickin' them up.'

The armoured car started up again. They listened as the sound grew faint, then was no longer heard. The IRA man at the window let the blind drop back. 'Shsh,' he said. 'Nobody move till we get the word.'

The fat guard, holding Dillon, relaxed his grip. Kev's high-pitched voice whispered, 'What are they lookin' for?'

No one answered him. Then, in a clear conversational voice, Moira said, 'You're scared out of your skins, aren't you?'

Beside him on the sofa Dillon felt Kev struggle with her, heard her gasp as Kev stopped her speech. The fat guard jammed his gun into Dillon's ear. 'Don't fuckin' move.'

A third voice, the voice of the man at the window, said, 'It's OK now.' A flashlight shone on Moira. Kev had his hand over her mouth and his other hand on her throat as if to choke her.

'Let her go,' the other IRA man said. The room light came on. The IRA man who had said, 'Let her go,' was the one Dillon had glimpsed briefly earlier, in the garden. Kev took his hand off Moira's mouth and allowed her to sit up. She coughed and massaged her neck. The other IRA man went to the door and opened it. 'Wait for the radio,' he said. 'It's not all clear yet.'

He went out, closing the door. Moira, still coughing, turned to Dillon as though they were alone in the room. 'Well, it's the truth, isn't it?' she said.

'Shut up, you!' Kev said. Suddenly, unable to contain himself, he slapped her, the force of the blow snapping her head back. At once as though he knew Dillon was going to hit him he turned and punched Dillon in the face with his closed fist. 'The pair of you, shut up.'

Dillon, his eyes stinging from the pain of the blow, moved across the sofa to comfort Moira. She sat, bolt upright, her slapped face reddened along the right cheek. When he touched her, she shook him off, moving to the far end of the sofa. 'I want a Kleenex,' she said. 'There are some in that drawer over there.'

The fat guard stood up, went to the place she had indicated and brought back a paper box of tissues. As he put it on the sofa beside her, he said, as if to no one in particular, 'There's no need for all this fightin'. There's no need for it.'

In the silence that followed Dillon thought of the hotel, of the night staff going home at eight, replaced by the morning shift of waiters, cleaners, the desk clerks moving into reception, the guests buying morning papers in the lobby, the line of people going into the dining-room for breakfast. In the past when the IRA planted bombs in hotels they always gave a warning. They had phoned in when they put a bomb in the Clarence kitchens last year. And in all the bombings of the Europa Hotel nobody had been hurt, had they? They were bombing property, not people. Calm down, he told himself. If they're going to bomb the hotel, it will be all right. It's only property. It will be all right.

But even as he told himself this he realised he did not know what they were going to do. It might not be the hotel at all. It might be something else.

Beside him, Moira blew her nose on a tissue. 'What time is it?' she asked him.

'I told you to shut up,' Kev said. 'Do you hear me? Shut up!'

'It's half six,' the fat guard said.

THREE

Light, faint at first, had ripened into the bold yellow tone of a summer's morning. It shone below the window blind, competing with the lamplight in the room. Shortly after seven, Kev switched off the lamp and raised the blind six inches from the bottom, allowing them a view of the avenue. Morning traffic could be heard on the nearby Antrim Road and, as they watched, a milk van came up the avenue, delivering bottles and collecting empties. As it did, the radio crackled in the hall outside and the tall youth came in, asking urgently, 'Did you order milk?'

Dillon looked at Moira who sat, her hands folded on her lap, staring down at her shoes, ignoring the question. He looked up at the masked face. 'We usually take a pint.' When he said that, the youth stepped to the window and pulled the blind down again. They waited in silence, hearing the footsteps of the milkman crossing the avenue, coming in their direction. There was the sound of their front gate opening, the chink of bottles, and the gate shut again. The van moved on.

The tall youth had eased the blind up to its former position, allowing a partial view of the avenue. 'Ten minutes,' he said cryptically to the others. He went out, closing the door.

Across the avenue, directly opposite their house, Mr Harbin-

48

son, a retired bank manager, came out of his front door, slipping a lead on his old Airedale dog. Dillon watched Mr Harbinson walk down the path to his front gate, open it, and stand on the pavement, raising his hand, palm open as though he had felt a spit of rain. Mr Harbinson looked up at the sky, unaware that he was being watched by armed men in woollen balaclava helmets. He shut his front gate and started off up the avenue, passing the white Ford, stopping as his dog lifted its leg to urinate on the low garden wall of a house two doors up from his own.

Mr Harbinson, like themselves, had probably never seen an IRA man in the flesh. There had never been demonstrations or Sinn Fein parades in this part of the city. Mr Harbinson was, by the sound of him, almost certainly a Protestant, but, equally likely, he was no more a religious Protestant than Dillon was a religious Catholic. Mr Harbinson would never fight a civil war to prevent Ulster from becoming a part of the Irish Republic, or take up arms to affirm his status as a citizen of the United Kingdom. Mr Harbinson, like ninety per cent of the people of Ulster, Catholic and Protestant, just wanted to get on with his life without any interference from men in woollen masks.

And now, watching him go off for his morning walk with his dog, Dillon felt anger rise within him, anger at the lies which had made this, his and Mr Harbinson's birthplace, sick with a terminal illness of bigotry and injustice, lies told over the years to poor Protestant working people about the Catholics, lies told to poor Catholic working people about the Protestants, lies from parliaments and pulpits, lies at rallies and funeral orations, and, above all, the lies of silence from those in Westminster who did not want to face the injustices of Ulster's status quo. Angry, he stared across the room at the most dangerous victims of these lies, his youthful, ignorant, murderous captors. What are they planning to do today, what new atrocity will they work at to keep us mired in hate?

Somewhere in the house a door banged. Kev stood up, flexing

his arms and legs as though stiff from sitting. He walked over to the sofa and, positioning himself directly in front of Moira, began to do knee bends. Moira turned sideways on the sofa, pulling down her skirt as though she thought he was trying to look up her legs. Kev inched himself closer, did half a dozen more knee bends, then rested on his hunkers, looking at her. She did not look at him. He stood, went to the table to get his revolver, stuck it in his belt, and said to the fat one, 'Ten minutes is up, wouldn't you say?'

The fat one nodded. Kev went to the window and again hunkered down, peering at the avenue outside through the opening of the blind. As he did, there was a tramp of feet in the hall as though many more people had come into the house. At once Kev jumped up, exchanging a look with the fat one. The door opened. The tall youth came in, followed by a masked IRA man not seen before. The tall youth pointed at Dillon. 'All right. Step outside.'

As Dillon rose to obey, Moira jumped up with him and caught hold of his arm. 'Michael, Michael, listen.'

'Don't worry,' he said to her. 'It will be all right.'

'It won't be all right,' she said. She pulled him to her, as if to stop him leaving.

'Come on, now, we have to get goin',' the tall youth said to him. Then, to Moira, 'Let go of him, will you?'

But she did not let go. 'They're going to kill you,' she said hysterically. 'They are, I know they are.'

'Nobody's goin' to kill him if he does what he's told,' the tall youth said, and nodded to Kev who at once caught hold of Moira from behind, jerking her backwards, breaking her embrace. At the same time the new IRA man caught Dillon's arm, twisting it up into the small of his back, causing him to bend over in pain.

'Michael?' Moira called out in a panicky voice, but at once Kev put his hand over her mouth, struggling with her, silencing her. The tall youth and the other IRA man pushed Dillon out into the hall, shutting the door behind them. Further down the hall Dillon saw two masked figures sitting at the kitchen table. The IRA man let go of his arm and the tall youth, pointing his revolver at him, said, 'You and me's goin' upstairs. No funny stuff, do you hear?'

As Dillon started up the stairs, the tall one followed him step by step. 'You're goin' to change, now. Where are your clothes?'

'In the bedroom.'

'OK. Come on.'

They entered the bedroom. Moira's discarded nightgown lay spread out like a dressmaker's pattern on the rumpled bed. On the dressing-table her many toilet articles were jumbled in untidy profusion. The room smelled of her scent and the open wardrobe revealed a long line of her dresses and racks of her shoes.

'Where are *your* clothes?'

He went to the far end of the wardrobe where his few suits were.

'Put on the clothes you'd be wearin' to work this mornin'. A suit and a tie, right?'

As he took off the clothes he had worn last night he looked out of the bedroom window. His little red Renault sat, still parked in the entryway outside the garden gate. So they had not taken it away. Wearing only his underpants, he went to the drawer where his shirts were.

'Wait a minute,' his captor said. 'You'd better shave.'

Naked, he went into the bathroom. As he lathered his face the masked, helmeted head moved into view in the mirror behind him. 'Hurry, now,' it said.

He took up the razor. He had always been nervous of shaving with somebody standing close to him, and now the sight of this menacing head behind his made him almost cringe, as though waiting for a blow. The hooded eyes watched as he shaved and wiped his face. He went back into the bedroom where, watched by his tall captor, he put on a white shirt, a blue tie and the suit he would normally wear, then went over to Moira's dressing-table and put his wallet, his comb and money in his pocket.

'Tidy up your hair,' the voice behind him said. He used his comb, watching his captor through the mirror.

'Sit down. You and me's goin' to have a wee talk.'

His mouth felt dry. He joined his hands together to still their trembling. Now they would tell him what it was they wanted him to do. He sat on Moira's dressing stool while his captor sat on the bed, his blue-jeaned bottom on Moira's nightgown.

'You're goin' to leave here now,' his captor said. 'It's just like any other day. You're goin' to work. You take your normal route, down the Antrim Road, and at Clifton Street you turn right at Upper Library Street. You go across town the usual way and up University Road. You go into the Clarence and park your car in your reserved parking space. You'll arrive at a certain time. We'll discuss that later. When you park the car, you don't go into the hotel. Do you hear me?'

He nodded, staring at the masked eyes which watched him.

'You don't go into the hotel. You go straight back to the security hut and out on to the street again. If they ask you any questions at the gate, you say you want to get somethin' at the wee shop across the street. You know the wee shop across the street, don't you? Murray's is the name of it.'

He nodded.

'You go into Murray's for a minute, just long enough to buy somethin', cigarettes, or somethin', and then you come out and, when you do, there'll be a green taxi cruisin' by. You signal to him. You'll get in and he'll drive you home. OK?'

'Is there a bomb in my car?'

His captor hesitated. His eyes, circled by the oblong woollen eyeholes of his helmet, blinked, then shut as though he were trying to remember something. When he opened them again, he stared at Dillon for a moment. Then his voice, flat and mechanical as though he were reciting a speech he had memor-ised, said, 'Yes, there is a bomb in the car. It's set to a time device. Your job is to park the car in its proper place and come out right away. You speak to nobody. If somebody speaks to you, you just say hello, good morning, or whatever. Now, if you do exactly what I tell you, when you come back here your wife will be waitin' for you.'

'So you're going to blow up the hotel?'

His captor shifted his buttocks on the bed, rucking up Moira's nightgown. 'Never you mind what we're goin' to do.'

'Are you going to give a warning?' He heard his voice go up a note as he asked the question. Easy, he told himself. You sound hysterical. 'I said, are you going to give a warning? There are hundreds of people in the hotel, the people I work with, and guests, tourists, innocent people.'

His masked captor stared at him. 'Never you mind what we're goin' to do. You do as you're told and your wife will be all right.'

'But you gave a warning other times,' Dillon said. 'When you bombed the Europa. And when you put a bomb in the Clarence last year, you phoned in a warning.'

'That's right.' The eyes behind the mask shifted slightly. 'Will you stop worryin' your head about things that are none of your business! This is our business. I'm not discussin' it with you. I'm just tellin' you. If anythin' goes wrong because of you, when you come back here to this house, your wife will be here. But she'll be dead.'

In the triptych mirror of Moira's dressing-table Dillon saw his own face: strange, stricken, stilled. His captor began to drum his gloved fingers on the thigh of his worn jeans. Below in the hall he heard faint voices. But, while he saw and heard these things, it was as though he had been given an anacsthetic and was going under. As in a dream he heard the muffled explosion of a revolver, saw Moira scream soundlessly, saw her fall as they shot her. His mind, pulling away from panic, skittered back to the only hope he had left. 'But you'll give a warning?' he said. 'They're innocent people.'

'We're not lookin' to kill innocent people,' his captor said.

'And by the same token we're not wantin' to kill your wife either. But, if it has to be done, we'll do it. Those volunteers downstairs will do a nut job on her. Now, come on. Are you ready?'

They went out on to the landing. At the foot of the stairs, watching him as he came down, were the two masked men he had seen earlier in the kitchen. When he reached the front hall the sitting-room door was open. Inside, Moira sat on the sofa, with Kev sitting facing her and the fat guard, squatting on his heels, peering out at the street. Moira turned her head, saw him, and jumped up as if to run out to him. But Kev at once blocked her.

Behind Dillon, the tall youth, watching, said, 'Let go of her for a minute.'

Released, she ran out into the hallway. 'What are they going to do?' she asked in a shaky voice.

The tall youth said, 'Say goodbye to her now.'

And there in the hallway of this house he had planned to leave today for ever, watched by five masked and armed men, he held to him this girl he had wanted to leave, felt her body tremble, felt her fingers dig into his back. 'God take care of you,' she said, as though it were a prayer.

'I'll be back soon,' he told her. 'Take it easy, will you? Don't do anything silly. Promise me?'

'Good advice,' said the tall one. He tapped Dillon on the shoulder. 'Come on, now.'

But Moira held him, pressing him to her, forcing him to disengage himself from her grip. 'I won't be long,' he said.

'What are you going to do?'

'None of your business,' the tall youth said. He turned to Kev. 'Take her inside.'

Kev and the fat guard took hold of Moira's arms. 'Oh, Jesus,' she said, and began to sob.

'Come on, you.' The tall youth poked his gun in Dillon's back and led him down the hall and into the kitchen.

As he went, he heard Kev's voice say to her, 'Get inside!' *He is the one who would like to hurt her. He is the one who will kill her.*

In the kitchen, the tall youth stood facing him, while the other two masked men went to the back door, as if waiting for a signal. The tall youth looked at his digital watch and said, 'Volunteer, what time do you have on you?'

One of the men pulled back his shirtsleeves and looked at his wrist. 'Seven-thirty-five.'

'OK. Check outside,' said the tall one.

One of the masked men opened the back door and went out into the garden. He came in again. 'All clear.'

The tall one then put his hand on Dillon's shoulder in a parody of friendliness. 'Now, here's what you're goin' to do. Drive to the hotel, as I told you. When you get there it'll be just about eight. Don't stop anywhere on the way, don't try any funny stuff. Remember, you're bein' followed. We're in radio contact. One wrong move from you and somebody back here will blow her head off. Right?'

Dillon nodded. His mouth was dry.

'You'll not be stopped. There's no police checks on your route this mornin'. We're watchin' out for that. You'll not be searched at hotel security, you never are. The trunk of your car is locked. Don't try to open it. If you're not out of the hotel car-park five minutes after you go in, we'll know you double-crossed us. And one last thing.' The hand tightened on Dillon's shoulder. 'When the police ask you questions about us, we're all wearin' masks, you don't know names, or what we look like, nothin'. Remember, we'll know what you told them. And that goes for that wife of yours. If you value her life, you'll make sure she keeps her mouth shut. I've been hearin' about some of the remarks she passed last night. We know now she's an enemy of Ireland. She needn't think that bein' a Catholic from the Falls is goin' to save her neck. So, mind what you say, the pair of you.'

His gloved hand shot up as if to strike Dillon who instinctively flinched. But instead of a blow Dillon's car keys were thrown at him. He caught them. The tall youth turned to the back door. 'Volunteer?'

At the door, a second masked face nodded. 'All clear.'

The tall one gave Dillon a slight push, saying, 'On your way now. Be quick.'

The one at the back door opened it. He stepped outside into the morning sun and looked left and right to the other back gardens on either side. There was no one in sight. As he went along the garden path past bushes and flowerbeds, he saw an empty beer bottle beneath the old picnic table, a bottle left over from the picnic lunch he had eaten there with Moira last Sunday. He was being watched. Coming up to the garden gate he saw the fuchsia bush and, below it, Teddy's body, a small bag of fur and bones, the crushed skull clotted with blood. Flies were at it already.

When he opened the back gate it made a squealing sound. Three gardens up from his, a woman came out to put rubbish in her dustbin. She was dressed only in a cotton nightgown and when she heard the gate squeal, embarrassed at being seen undressed, she did not say good morning, but hurried back inside her house.

His car was where he had left it. Or was it? He thought it was parked a little way back from his usual place. It was locked. He turned the key in the door and slipped into the front seat, looking around for signs of change. The worn black upholstery, the box of tissues on the dashboard, the broken sunglasses in the gearbox tray, nothing seemed to have been touched. He listened but heard no ticking sound. When he put the key in the ignition he thought of films he had seen where cars exploded when the ignition was turned on. But the engine came to life and turned over quietly.

He drove out of the entryway into the avenue. The white Ford was still parked opposite his house. As he drove past it, going towards the Antrim Road, he saw the man in the driver's seat and the girl beside him. Both were looking in the other direction to avoid his seeing their faces. But he had seen their faces last night. Especially the girl's.

When he turned on to the Antrim Road, the white Ford was following him. His route would take him from North to South Belfast, through streets little changed since his childhood. He would skirt the boundaries of poor working-class areas and drive past the large monuments and buildings at the city's centre. It was a route which on a normal day was far too familiar to evoke in him any thought of what he was passing. But this morning, in a car which was a moving bomb, followed by terrorists who could radio in an order to kill his wife, he was driving for what might be the last time through this ugly, troubled place which held for him implacable memories of his past life. Now, in ironic procession, he would pass the house where he had been born, the boarding school in which he had been a pupil, and the university where he had written poetry, edited a student magazine, and dreamed of another life.

The house came first, at a turn in the road, not half a mile from where he now lived. It was larger than the houses which adjoined it, aloof in its own grounds with, at the back, a tennis court, a lawn, a vegetable garden, the whole surrounded by a high hedge which hid it from the surrounding streets.

It had been his grandfather's house, his grandfather who had started the family tradition of running hotels, his grandfather who had begun down on the docks with a pub and rooms to let above it and who, from that beginning, had made himself into A. D. Dillon, Importer of Wines & Spirits, owning two small hotels and supplying drink to a dozen pubs. His grandfather, who had died before Dillon was born, was known to him only as a figure in a family photograph. Bearded and broad-beamed like Edward VII, he was shown standing by a large Daimler car, on the running board of which sat his three children, dressed in sailor suits.

The house was called Ardath. Dillon's father had moved back into it in 1947, the year his grandfather died. Dillon was born

57

there five years later and lived in the house until he was ten, when his feckless father sold it to buy Kinsallagh, a large country house in Donegal, which he turned into a hotel. He remembered his father playing tennis in long white trousers on the old grass court: he remembered the greenhouse which was always warm and where he watched frogspawn turn into frogs. Now, as he drove past, he could still see the old name 'ARDATH' on a stone plinth at the right-hand side of the gate. But a newer sign on the left read 'Sisters of Mercy: School for Girls'.

He drove on, passing the cinema where as a boy he had watched films in which men fired revolvers at other men and bombs blew up forts and other buildings, but where, always, in the end, the bad men paid for their crimes. It was now a quarter to eight. What if the bomb went off too soon?

He stopped the car at a pedestrian crossing. A young woman, pushing her baby in a pram, moved on to the crossing, and, halfway across, turned and smiled at him. At once, irrationally, he felt a sense of panic. Hurry up. Get away from me. He looked in his rear-view mirror but a heavy lorry loaded with aluminium milk cans had moved in behind him, so that he could not see the white Ford. When the girl and her baby reached the other side of the street, he drove on and at that moment saw the white Ford move up, passing the lorry, to pull in again at his rear.

Suddenly, three little boys, whirling their school satchels in the air as if to attack each other, ran across the street, shouting and laughing in the middle of traffic. They wore navy blazers and white shirts, with the tie of his school knotted like frayed rope-ends around their necks. Ignoring the squealing brakes around them, they gained the opposite pavement and continued their helter-skelter chase. Ahead, to his right, he could see the ornamental iron gates, the long tree-lined avenue and, at its end, the red brick façade of the Catholic school where for eleven years he had been a boarder, a school where teaching was carried on by bullying and corporal punishment and learning by rote, a school run by priests whose narrow sectarian views perfectly propagated the divisive bitterness which had led to the events of last night.

Look at me, look at me, he wanted to shout as he drove past those hated gates. See this car on its way to kill innocent people, see my wife in a room with a gun at her head, and then ask your Cardinal if he can still say of these killers that he can see their point of view.

He drove into the roundabout at Carlisle Circus. In its centre was a stone plinth which had once supported the statue of a Protestant divine, a statue like many of the city's monuments, toppled in the war and never replaced. The white Ford came circling around behind him as he entered Clifton Street and drove past the headquarters of the Orange Order, that fount of Protestant prejudice against the third of Ulster's people who are Catholics. Above the ugly grey stone building was a statue which had not been toppled by war or civil strife, a Dutch prince on horseback, waving a sword, staring out over the damaged city at ancient unchanging Irish hills, a statue commemorating a battle three hundred years ago in which the forces of the Protestant House of Orange defeated, on Irish soil, the forces of a Papist English king. At the bottom of Clifton Street he turned right, driving along the edge of those Protestant and Catholic ghettos which were the true and lasting legacy of this British Province founded on inequality and sectarian hate. In ten minutes he would reach the Clarence. And then what would he do?

If the car were to break down now, here in this street, he would have to get out and try to start it up, knowing that the people in the white Ford were behind him, watching him. Parking was strictly forbidden in these central streets, so, within minutes, the police would come along to ask what was wrong. At that moment the people in the white Ford might radio a signal to the house. Moira could be shot. Besides, these streets were full of people. If the bomb went off here, dozens of them might be killed. If it went off in the hotel, after a phone warning, perhaps there would be no loss of life?

59

He drove on, passing the large Victorian buildings in Fisher-wick Place, moving in the line of morning traffic which went towards Shaftesbury Square. How many minutes after he parked the car in the hotel would it be before the bomb went off? What if the warning was phoned in too late? But they had not promised to give a warning. They promised nothing. The bomb could be set to go off as little as ten minutes after he parked the car. Even if he did tell the police, they might not be able to evacuate the hotel in time. And if he told the police Moira would be shot. And if the police were not able to evacuate the people in time the people in the hotel would be killed. And he would be the one who killed them.

Behind him, a car horn hooted impatiently. He realised his driving had slowed to a crawl and he was holding up the line of traffic now coming up to a green light. He was approaching the entrance gates and grounds of Queen's University. The pavements were crowded with students in rented gowns converging, with their families and friends, on the graduation cere-monies. Today these students will be given passports to a new life. He had been one of them once, hoping to find a teaching job in England, but ready to go anywhere, Africa or the Middle East if it would get him away from here. He had worn that rented gown, he had sat in Whitla Hall waiting for his name to be called: 'Michael Patrick Dillon, Second Class Honours, English', waiting to walk to centre stage where some English captain of industry stood in his chancellorial robes, ready to shake his hand and give him his degree.

And afterwards he had hurried along this road to the Clarence, laughing and joking with his friends, flirting with the girls, ready for a celebratory booze-up, seeing himself as a coming poet, pleased with his success. He had not known then that degree day was not a passport to freedom, but the end of freedom. He had not found the teaching job he wanted in England, in Europe, or in some faraway exotic place. His grandfather had run pubs and a hotel, his father ran a hotel and he had ended up, like them, a servant of sorts, arranging to feed people and pour their drinks and provide beds for them. Unlike his father and grandfather, he did not even own the hotel which he was now on his way to destroy.

At the main gates of the university he stopped to let a graduating party cross the street. The new graduate came first, pretty in her rented gown, her legs attractive in black stockings and patent leather pumps. Behind her, her parents, dressed in their best, and her brother and sister, making jokes, all of them proud of the one who was now adding a small cubit to their family's stature. In a few hours, joyous and triumphant, they would head up the road to the Clarence for a festive lunch. Or would they?

It depended on him.

The white Ford had followed him, always three car-lengths to the rear, but as he turned into the Malone Road he saw it veer off and disappear. Did they have someone inside the hotel, waiting for his arrival? It could be anyone, staff, a guest, or even someone who had come in to have breakfast in the dining-room. One thing was certain. He was still being watched.

Ahead now was a sign:

THE CLARENCE HOTEL
BAR-RESTAURANT

He stopped the car opposite the sign, waiting for a break in traffic which would allow him to turn into the hotel entrance. At the entrance, lined up at the security gates, was a queue of four cars. He watched the oncoming traffic and when he saw his chance swung his car across the road and joined this queue. For a moment he thought of surreptitiously signalling to one of the security men and telling him to detain the car for inspection. But the IRA knew the guards never inspected his car. And what if a guard opened the trunk and the bomb exploded here at the gate?

Billy Craig, a retired policeman, dressed as usual in a black police sweater with black-leather elbow pads, was in charge of the security team which checked over incoming cars. A car had just been cleared and was moving towards the gates. Billy hobbled forward to open up but, just then, saw Dillon's little red Renault join the queue. At once he held up his hand officiously, stopping the other car and waving Dillon on through. As Dillon's car passed, Billy called out, 'Morning, sir.'

Dillon waved to him. The area in front of the hotel's main entrance was used only for pick-up and delivery of guests and luggage. As he drove past the entrance, going around to the visitors' car-park in the rear of the hotel, he saw that the main lobby was crowded with people. In the car-park at the rear there were four spaces reserved for the senior staff. His space was just below the windows of the Emerald Room, one of the banqueting-rooms adjoining the main restaurant. The car-park was already crowded and a tour bus, waiting for a French group, was stationed awkwardly in the centre. He had seen the French group in the dining-room last night, middle-aged teachers and civil servants from Brittany, anxiously studying the strange menu, prudently choosing to drink beer instead of the overpriced wine.

He manoeuvred the Renault around the tour bus. Just beyond the bus, two cars had moved into vacant parking places, and now in a flurry of opening doors their occupants were getting out. They were locals, middle-aged men with that bluff quick Ulster way of walking. Two of them, younger than the others, wore electric-blue jogging suits, and as Dillon drove up they stepped in front of his car with hard stares, as though he had just made an illegal parking move. One put up his hand, signalling him to stop. Dillon obeyed, surprised, and, as he did, the other passengers came out from between the cars, four men in dark clothes surrounding a tall, elderly figure who was wearing an ill-fitting grey suit and a celluloid clerical collar. As the old man came out, shielded by the others, the young men in jogging suits moved on in front of him, hurrying towards the hotel's rear entrance.

The tall old man was now directly approaching Dillon's car. His face, weathered by the rain and wind of a lifetime of open-air meetings, had the staring vacant look of a gargoyle on some cathedral buttress. When he was directly in front of Dillon's car, he turned and waved to him, absently, as though he was the grand marshal in a parade. His minders, the young men in jogging suits, were now at the hotel's side entrance, holding open the doors.

Dillon did not wave back. The old man lumbered on towards the hotel door. He watched him, the Reverend Alun Pottinger, the 'mad dog of Protestant Ulster', as his enemies called him, going in to a breakfast for his overseas supporters, a breakfast at which he would deliver his usual sermon of religious hatred. The way was now clear for Dillon to park his car. As he moved it into his allotted space he looked up at the windows of the Emerald Room above him. Sitting at a dozen tables in the room were men and women who were not locals. They looked like Americans. They were, he realised, the Canadian Orange Order supporters who had come to hear Pottinger speak.

He switched off the ignition. His heart beat irregularly as though it belonged in some other body. He looked again at the window which faced him. The head table was right by the window. It was not yet filled. As he watched, Pottinger and his group arrived in the room. People stood up to applaud, as, shaking hands, Pottinger moved through the room and, after a moment of consultation, took his place at the centre of the head table, less than twenty feet above Dillon's parked car.

Dillon stared at Pottinger's back as Pottinger sat down. The minders in jogging suits moved up to the window. One of them stood, looking down at him. And, watching him, Dillon knew. The IRA are not bombing the hotel. I am here to kill Pottinger. There will be no warning. The bomb will go off very soon.

But why would they want to kill Pottinger? They had never tried to kill him before. It was said Pottinger's anti-Catholic rantings were the greatest propaganda benefit the IRA ever had. But they had picked this parking spot, they had picked this day, this time. They said, 'If you're not out of the hotel car-park five minutes after you go in, we'll know you double-crossed us.' If I get out of the car now and walk away, Pottinger and his Canadian friends will be blown sky high. And I will have killed him.

The minder kept looking down at him. Dillon took his keys from the ignition and got out of the car. As he walked away from his parking space he passed the windows of the main restaurant which adjoined the Emerald Room. The lower sashes of the windows were open, for the morning was warm. He heard people speaking French. He looked up, listening to that tongue he had learned. At a table beside the window one of the tourists, a grey-haired woman in her fifties, was telling the others that today's breakfast was included in the price of the hotel room, but that lunch, later, at the Giant's Causeway, would be an extra charge. An old man with a thick Breton accent said that they should all eat up, because this breakfast where you got eggs, bacon and good bread was probably better than the food they would be offered for lunch.

Dillon stared at the old man. You will never eat lunch again. By lunch-time, most of your group will be dead. Tonight, television pictures will show the bomb damage done in this hotel. Tomorrow, newspapers in Brest or Dinard may run your photographs and interview those few of you who survive. But for the rest of the world it will be the Reverend Pottinger's photograph which will be seen in the Press. You will be killed by people who do not know you, who will never see you, who do not care if you live or die. Your friends at home may have warned you that it is dangerous to come here. It is no more dangerous than crossing a street in Dinard, but that small statistic will not help you now.

He stood, staring. They were schoolteachers, civil servants, small business people. They had families in France who depended on them. He looked back at the windows of the Emerald

Room where Pottinger's Canadian supporters had begun to applaud. They, too, have families who depend on them.

And I have Moira. Moira, who I planned to leave.

He turned away from the window and walked out of the car-park, passing the hotel's front entrance. I am going away from the phone. Is there a phone in Murray's shop? Do I still have a chance to ring the police?

Jack, a uniformed doorman, came down from the main entrance carrying a departing guest's suitcases. 'Mornin', Mr Dillon.'

'Morning, Jack.'

'Big day coming up,' Jack said.

'It will be that, all right.'

He walked on, going down the driveway towards the security gates. All at once he had the feeling that he was being followed. He looked back. A delivery boy, who could not have been more than twelve or thirteen years old, was walking some thirty paces behind him, carrying a floral arrangement in a wicker basket. When he looked at the boy the boy stopped and pretended to rearrange his flowers. He could be an IRA lookout. It was said they used children for these jobs.

The security gates were closed so, to save time, he walked through the security hut to reach the street. The guards were doing a careful search of car occupants this morning, going over them in a strict body check. Pottinger's presence in the hotel would be the reason for that. He looked at his watch as he came out on to the Malone Road. It was eight-thirty-five. He had been inside exactly seven minutes.

Traffic was heavy on the Malone Road. There was no sign of the white Ford. At the taxi rank outside the hotel, four taxis waited in a queue. None of them was green. The delivery boy came out into the street and, ignoring Dillon, went off in the direction of Shaftesbury Square.

Two streets away the traffic lights went red, halting the flow of cars and allowing Dillon to cross the road. Why did they ask me to go into Murray's and buy something? Is it to give them time to bring the taxi up?

He looked back at the hotel. At the far end of the street the delivery boy, still holding his floral basket, was talking to a tall girl who wore a long yellow muffler wrapped around her neck, although the morning was warm. They were not looking at him. He walked on and pushed open the door of the little shop. It sold newspapers, sweets and cigarettes and had four rows of shelves lined with tinned goods, dairy items and cold meats for sandwiches. There were three people waiting to pay for their purchases at the lone check-out counter. As he opened the door of the shop he saw the girl in the yellow muffler crossing the street behind him, coming in his direction.

It is happening. It is happening just as they planned it. We are all part of the team, I, the delivery boy, that girl, the people in the white Ford, the masked ones at my house. The bomb is in place. It will go off any minute now. I have one more thing to do. Buy something here, cigarettes, sweets, so that they will have time to bring the taxi up. When I get in the green taxi it will all be over.

The people in the check-out queue moved forward. He looked around the shop. He saw no pay phone. He looked out of the shop window. The girl in the yellow muffler was standing outside on the pavement, her back to him. Suddenly, in a rush, he pushed past the people in the check-out line and leaned over the woman at the cash register. She looked up at him, a stout, red-faced woman with bad teeth.

'Is there a phone in here somewhere?' he said. 'Please, it's an emergency.'

She looked at the other people in the queue, then looked at him. 'There's a phone in that wee room back there. That wee office. Go ahead.'

He ran down the aisles of tinned goods. At the far end of the store was a white door, its upper panel clear glass. Inside, he saw rows of shelves, a jumble of cartons on the floor, and in the

66

middle of the room a cluttered desk with a phone on it. He pushed the door open. He picked up the receiver. In that instant it was as though he heard the flat Belfast voice say, *Do a nut job on her.* Trembling, he looked back at the door. Framed in the glass panel, staring in at him, was the girl in the yellow muffler. At once he bent over and dialled 999. He looked again as the phone began to ring. She was gone.

On the third ring a voice said, 'Belfast Central.'

'I want to report a bomb.'

'One moment.'

There was a click and a new voice answered. 'Right. Where are you?'

'I'm in a shop called Murray's across the road from the Clarence Hotel. The bomb is in my car in the hotel car-park. I left it there about eight minutes ago.' Suddenly he realised they would think he was an IRA man. 'I'm the hotel manager,' he said. 'The IRA put the bomb in my car and made me drive it there. They're holding my wife at home. They're going to kill her because I'm phoning you. They're watching me now.'

The voice was calm, quick. 'What's your home address?'

He gave it. The voice said the police would be on their way to his house immediately. It told him to go back to the hotel, give a bomb alarm and evacuate the hotel at once. It asked where was his car exactly, what make was it, did he know where the bomb was hidden in it, and what was his name.

The voice then said, 'Look, Mr Dillon, they may phone in a warning to the hotel. Usually, they just want to damage the hotel.'

'No. I didn't tell you. Alun Pottinger's giving a speech in the hotel. He's there now and my car is parked just under the window of the room he's speaking in.'

'Go back to the hotel at once. Do what I said and wait for us at the front door. We're on our way.'

He put the receiver down. He stood in that small room, amid the jumble of cartons printed with the names of food items, looking down at the small desk, littered with bills, a Rolodex file, a pair of spectacles, a tabloid newspaper, open at a photograph of a girl smiling up at him, holding her hands over her naked breasts. Above him, growing louder as it stationed itself in the sky above the Malone Road, training its spy cameras on the streets below, the corncrake chatter of a British Army surveillance helicopter drowned out all other sounds. Was it coincidence, or could the response to his alarm be so sudden?

He pushed open the door of the little storeroom and ran out into the shop. He saw no sign of the girl in the yellow muffler. The few customers in the shop went on with their purchases, impervious to the familiar racket in the sky. The woman at the check-out called, 'All right, love?' as he waved to her and ran out into the street. He rushed into the oncoming traffic, holding his hand up like a policeman as he skipped across to the other side. He ran towards a queue of cars at the security gates, calling to Billy, 'Open the gates, get rid of those cars. Bomb scare.'

Billy pulled the gate open and he ran through it, winded now as he rushed up to the hotel's front entrance. He ran across to reception and told Maggie Donlon, 'Put it on the speaker. We're evacuating the hotel. Put on the fire alarms. Have someone check all the rooms. Hurry.'

'What is it, Michael?'

'A bomb.'

As he spoke he heard police sirens outside, impatient at being stalled in traffic. He ran back to the front door. Two police armoured cars were coming through the gates, hooting at other cars to move aside. Behind him, he heard Maggie's voice on the public address system. 'Everyone must leave the hotel at once. Leave the hotel at once.' The fire alarm bells began their shrill, trilling sound. People were beginning to pass him, going out of the front doors of the hotel. They were, surprisingly, not pushing or running. He heard voices behind him asking, 'Is it a fire? It must be a fire.'

The first police armoured car pulled up with a jerk in front of the hotel. He raised his hand, signalling, as four policemen, armed and in flak jackets, tumbled out of the rear of the car, advancing on him. 'Are you the manager?'

'Yes. The car's in the car-park at the back. I'll show you.'

'Where's Dr Pottinger?'

'In the banqueting-room,' he said, surprised.

'Take us there, will you?'

When the police ran in at the revolving doors, Jack, the doorman, was pinning the panels back to allow the stream of people to get out. Dillon, with the police at his heels, ran through the lobby, raising stares from the exiting guests as he and the police rushed into the banqueting-room corridor. Coming towards him, hurrying, were the two minders in blue jogging suits and behind, flanked by his four assistants, the tall, scare-crow figure of Pottinger. The police, recognising Pottinger, at once surrounded him, clearing a way as they hurried him through the lobby. 'This way, Reverend. Quick, now.'

'What is it, what's up, is it a bomb scare?'

Dillon, forgotten, stood watching them go. The fire alarms sounded again and again. The public address voice repeated, 'The hotel is being evacuated. Everyone must leave at once.'

Suddenly, a police sergeant, leading a second team of heavily armed policemen, stood in front of Dillon. 'You're Mr Dillon? Right. Where's the car?' And they were off again, running to the rear entrance which led from the dining-rooms to the car-park at the back of the hotel.

The French tour bus was still blocking the car-park exit. People were running to get to their cars but the police shooed them off. 'No time,' they called. 'Get out of here.'

The sergeant turned to him. 'Which one?'

He pointed. 'That one. The Renault.' The sergeant pulled out a short-wave radio and spoke into it. Dillon did not hear what he said. The bomb would go off at any moment. He wanted to run out of the car-park.

The sergeant shouted to one of the other policemen, 'Get that bus out of here.'

As the policeman ran towards it, Dillon saw the French tourists coming into the car-park, heard the French voices, confused, alarmed. 'C'est une incendie? Non, il dit que c'est une bombe.' The tourists began to hurry towards their bus, but the driver, with a policeman directing him, swung the bus around and drove out of the car-park, leaving the tourists panicky, abandoned, in this foreign place.

He ran towards them, telling them in French to hurry down to the gates, forget about the bus, hurry, quickly, quickly. Their faces stared at him, and then they turned away, frightened, obeying him.

He looked at his car. There was a policeman standing near it. The policeman seemed afraid. The sergeant and the other two policemen were running around clearing the car-park of people. He looked at his watch. It was almost nine. By now, if things had gone as the bombers planned, Pottinger's audience would have finished their bacon and eggs and Pottinger would be on his feet, beginning to speak. He looked at the little red Renault, sitting empty under the Emerald Room windows and, turning away, hurried after the French tourists, ignoring the police sergeant who seemed to have forgotten him. As he did, amid the shrill fire alarms, the shouts, the clatter of the surveillance helicopter above, he heard a new sound of sirens. Two Army Land Rovers raced into the car-park. Soldiers tumbled out of both vehicles as they slammed to a stop. An officer with the rank of captain spoke to the police sergeant who, turning, called, 'Mr Dillon. You're wanted here.'

He went back. The officer was waiting for him. The police sergeant pointed to the Renault. The officer came up to Dillon and asked in brisk British tones, 'Your car? Did you see them place the bomb?'

He shook his head. 'No, but they said it's in the trunk.'

'This is the ATO,' the police sergeant said. 'He's in charge now.'

The officer ignored this. He asked what time the car had been parked in the car-park, then told Dillon, 'All right, clear out.' He turned to the police. 'You too. Is everybody out of those rooms?' He pointed to the banqueting-room windows, and then, not waiting for his question to be answered, he walked away, going towards the Land Rovers which, Dillon saw, were filled with special equipment.

'All right, let's get out of here,' the police sergeant said to Dillon. He, the three other policemen and Dillon all began to run towards the exit to the car-park. Running, Dillon looked back at the scene he was leaving: the soldiers moving cautiously towards the Renault, the Land Rovers parked in the middle of the car-park, the officer supervising the unloading of some device.

At the front of the hotel, the last evacuees were being hurried towards the street. Dillon saw Collis, the banquet manager, standing in the front doorway, shouting to two waiters to hurry up. Maggie Donlon, who had been at reception, was half-carrying an old woman who was still in her nightdress.

He ran up to Maggie. 'Are they all out?'

'I believe so, yes.'

He turned back, panicky again, waving to Collis to hurry up. Collis nodded and came to join him. 'Is everybody out?' he said to Collis.

'All my lot are out,' Collis said. 'I hear it's a real fuckin' bomb this time.'

'It is that,' he said.

The security hut was deserted; the gates lay open. As they went towards the Malone Road he could see what seemed like hundreds of people crowding the pavements, staring up at the hotel. Overhead, the surveillance helicopter still clattered out its deafening noise. Fire engines, their sirens dying as they arrived, moved up to the entrance, scattering the watching crowds. A police armoured car, the last car to leave the hotel, came careening down the driveway and stopped close to Dillon. A policeman jumped out of the car and ran over to the sergeant. Dillon heard their radios crackling, heard the sergeant say, 'No, Pottinger's out. We had him out ten minutes ago.'

He went to the sergeant, gripping his arm. 'Is that your headquarters you're phoning? Will you ask about my wife? What about my wife?'

'What *about* your wife?' the sergeant said, puzzled. 'Where is she?'

'The IRA are holding her in our house.'

'Wait.' The sergeant turned and walked a few paces away as if he did not want Dillon to hear what he was saying. Dillon saw him speak into the receiver.

Suddenly, the ground shook; an intense vibration preceded all sound. Then with a rumbling roar like a wall collapsing the car-park behind the hotel set up a great cloud of dust and debris. All around Dillon people ducked down as though cowering from the lash of a great whip. In the seconds after the explosion a quiet filled the street, a quiet which ended with voices, strange at first as the twittering of birds. 'The bomb – it's a bomb, oh, my God, was anybody, is anybody still in there?'

Maggie Donlon's pale face appeared in front of him, her hand gripping his wrist. 'Are the soldiers still in there?'

'Yes.' He turned to the police sergeant who stood holding his radio against his chest as if to protect it. 'What happened?'

'Maybe they blew it up,' the sergeant said. 'Or it blew itself up, more likely. It's OK. Those fellas know their job.' He seemed irritated at being interrupted. Again, he turned away, tuning his radio which was giving off static. He listened, raising his hand, warning Dillon to be quiet.

All around people babbled on in the alarmed excited tones of survivors. 'We weren't out five minutes,' someone was saying. 'Five more minutes and we'd all have been dead.'

Other voices called out, worried. 'Did you see Helen? Is Helen with you?'

'It's the IRA.'

'It was a bomb.'

'Was anybody up in the rooms?'

'No, she's here. I saw her a minute ago.'

'It blew up in the back somewhere. It was at the back of the hotel.'

The sergeant, switching off his radio, beckoned to Dillon, drawing him away from Maggie Donlon and the other spectators. As Dillon followed the sergeant's flak-jacketed back, a sick ball of fear and certainty filled his stomach. *She's dead.* The sergeant pushed his way through a knot of waiting people and stood by the hood of his armoured vehicle. When Dillon joined him he put his hand on Dillon's shoulder and said in a low confidential tone, 'I have a message for you. No, no, it's not about your wife. But I'm to advise you to tell nobody about your part in this – about your car – and the bomb – not a word, do you understand? It's for your own protection.'

'But what about my wife, is she all right?'

'They're dealing with that. I'm sorry I've no definite news for you yet.'

'Why not?' Dillon asked wildly, but did not wait for an answer. He turned and pushed his way through to the place where Maggie Donlon was still standing. 'Maggie, do you have your car with you? Where is it parked?'

'Down on Wellesley Avenue. The usual place. Do you want to borrow it? It's a wee yellow Fiat.'

'Give me the keys. It's an emergency.'

She stared at him as she took the keys from her purse. 'Are you all right, Michael? What's up?'

He shook his head, unable to speak. He took the keys and, pushing his way past the gawking spectators, ran out into the road, in among the cars which cruised slowly past the hotel, their occupants staring at the fire engines, the cloud of dust, the crowds. Running like a thief in the middle of the road amid hooting horns, he reached Wellesley Avenue and Maggie's car. When he drove the car out on to University Road, he rejoined the stalled traffic which was now moving in a slow stream towards the university grounds. He sat, gripping the wheel, his heart beating a loud panic as he inched forward towards the main gates and the graduation ceremonies.

They're dealing with that, the sergeant said. Dealing with what? Moving Moira's body out of the house? Or are they surrounding the house, waiting to go in and find out what happened?

Once past the university he was able to speed up, driving back along the same route he had taken to come here this morning. He drove erratically. He saw Kev's masked face, heard his high angry voice, saw the gloved hand pointing the revolver. Kev didn't kill her. I killed her. I killed her when I picked up the phone, I killed her to save those French tourists, I killed her to save Pottinger and those bigots in the Emerald Room.

He drove around Carlisle Circus and on to the Antrim Road. Ahead of him, a traffic light went red. He drove through it. He almost hit a man who stepped off the pavement as he ran the light. Car horns sounded on either side of him as he overtook traffic, weaving in and out, the road in front of him unreal, half noticed, as, vivid and startling, he saw Moira on her wedding day, holding him in an embrace in the caterer's tent, whispering, 'Till death do us part; do you believe that?'

Yes, he said, yes, of course he did.

And then she said, in a phrase that warned him that Moira Keenan, now his wife, was a stranger he did not know, 'I believe it too. I know I won't make old bones. I don't want to get old and ugly and nobody will look at me any more. I'm going to die young when men still want me. While I have the power.'

And what had he said to that, some joke, he supposed? He did not remember. But now, driving back, expecting to find her dead, he wondered if it was the most poignant thing she had ever told him about her life.

74

Three streets from Winchester Avenue, he began to look for roadblocks, police, crowds. But it was like any other morning on the Antrim Road. People were out, strolling, shopping, bringing small children to the park, as though they were residents of a city thousands of miles away from bombs and guns. For most of them, these IRA events were what they saw on television, items on a daily disaster list of airline crashes, hostage crises in the Middle East, guerrilla wars, highjackings. Even now, walking on the Antrim Road, none of them would ever think that masked men with guns and bombs might have been in their midst this morning.

Winchester Avenue was next left. Sick with tension he put on his turn signal. As he drove into the avenue, two armed policemen standing on the corner looked him over. They did not stop him. Ahead, halfway up the avenue, he saw an armoured police car parked outside his house. At the very top of the avenue a second police car waited at the intersection. When he saw that he had been allowed through, he guessed that the IRA were no longer in the house. The police are in the house now, with Moira. *Dead?*

He parked his car near the armoured police car. As he got out he saw that there was an ordinary car parked just ahead of the police car. A man in civilian clothes was sitting in the driver's seat. A doctor? The man did not look at him as he passed by. When he unlatched the front gate and went up the path, the front door opened as though he was expected. A policeman in flak jacket stood at the opened door. 'I'm Michael Dillon,' Dillon said.

The policeman nodded and beckoned him in. 'Just don't touch anything, will you, sir?' the policeman said. 'There'll be a team here shortly to go over the place.'

He followed the policeman's pointing finger and went into the front sitting-room. As he did, a man rose to greet him, a neat-looking man in his forties, wearing a white shirt, red wool

75

tie and a blue business suit. Behind him, sitting on the sofa, was Moira.

'Oh, God,' Dillon said, and went to her, embracing her, felt her skin warm against his cheek. Suddenly, he gasped as though he would begin to weep. He hugged her tight, then realised that she had not put her arms around him, had not returned his kiss. 'Are you all right?' he asked.

'She's OK,' a voice behind him said. 'We sent word back to the hotel to tell you, but you were gone already. By the way, I'm Detective Inspector Randall. Harry Randall. Your wife's had a great shock, of course. But, all's well that ends well. I gather there were no casualties back at the hotel?'

'I don't know,' he said. He looked at Moira. 'Are you all right?' he asked again.

She nodded, not looking at him.

'What happened?'

She did not answer. The Inspector said, 'What time did you leave here, Mr Dillon?'

'A quarter to eight.'

'Aye, well, they took off at about eight-twenty. They left Mrs Dillon in this room. They told her if she moved or did anything, you would be killed. So she was still here, waiting, when we came in at eight-forty-five.'

He stared at the Inspector. 'Then they left here before they knew I'd phoned?'

The Inspector nodded. He opened a small loose-leaf note-book, riffling its pages. Looking at him, Dillon was reminded of a bank manager considering a loan. 'Yes, that's right. You didn't ring up until eight-thirty-six. While we're at it, it would be a help if we try to get the picture clear. Your wife has told me, more or less, what happened here last night. Now, if you could tell me exactly what happened to you after you left here this morning?'

Moira looked at him suddenly, waiting.

And so, anxious, on trial, he sat beside her on the sofa and

76

told again of his drive through the city with the white Ford following him. He told of his arrival at the hotel, of seeing Pottinger in the car-park and realising that this was an assassination attempt. Turning to Moira, he told her how he had walked past the dining-room windows and watched the innocent French tourists eating inside. They listened in silence, she and the Inspector. They had become his judges. He told about the suspicious delivery boy and the girl in the yellow muffler. He told how, suddenly, in the little shop, he had phoned the police. 'I thought of those people,' he said to Moira. 'And, of course, all the time I was thinking about you.'

She looked at him. 'Were you?'

'And then what?' the Inspector said, as though to stifle her question.

'Then, on the phone, the police told me to go back to the hotel and give the alarm at once. And about ten minutes after that, the bomb went off. I don't know if the Army blew it up, or what.'

'The Army didn't blow it up,' the Inspector said. 'I'd assume it was set to go off at eight-fifty and it went off as planned.'

Dillon turned to Moira. 'Then, I got a car and came here.'

There was a silence which the Inspector hurried to fill. 'And you've told nobody about your part in this, Mr Dillon?'

'No, the police said not to.'

'Why?' Moira asked.

'It's for your own protection,' the Inspector said. 'If the IRA was trying to kill Dr Pottinger they won't want it known that they made a mess of it. They'll probably let people think it was a hotel bombing and that they were the ones who gave the warning to evacuate. So, it's better that you say nothing. I mean, if the media got hold of this story you'd get a lot of publicity and people would know you stood up to the IRA. That would put you at greater risk.'

'But we're at risk now,' Moira said. 'Aren't we?'

'That's right. There's no telling what they'll do. I think, under the circumstances, you know your options.'

'What options?' Moira said. 'What do you mean?'

'Well, we can't advise you, of course. But, in the past, there've been a few people in your situation, people who didn't do what they told them to do. Those people moved away. They left Ireland. Mind you, I'm not saying that anything is going to happen to you or Mr Dillon. What I'm saying is, we can't really protect you. We can't guarantee your safety.'

While the Inspector had been speaking, a police van had drawn up on the opposite side of the avenue. A few people had come out of their houses and now watched, curious, as policemen carrying boxes of some equipment came into the Dillons' front hall. The Inspector turned away from them, listening to the commotion in the hall. 'Is there anywhere you could go – just for a few hours? Our team is going to go over the house now. They won't make a mess, but they'll be here for a while.'

'They all wore gloves,' Moira said, suddenly getting up and pulling the window curtains against the faces which stared at them from across the street. 'You won't find anything.'

The Inspector also rose. 'Gloves aren't complete protection,' he said, smiling in his deferential manner. He turned to Dillon. 'I suppose you didn't, at any time, see any of their faces?'

'Yes, I did,' Dillon said. He saw Moira look at him, surprised.

'When was that?' the Inspector said.

'One of them, the one called Kev, pulled up his mask. He had his back to me, but I saw his face in the mirror. He was scratching his cheek. He had bad acne.'

'Does he know you saw him?'

'No.'

'That could be very useful, then,' the Inspector said. 'But I think it would be wise if neither of you mention this to anyone else. Except members of the police, of course. Now, I suppose you'll want to get back to the hotel, Mr Dillon. Mrs Dillon, can we give you a lift somewhere? I have my car and driver outside.'

'You could go to Peg Wilton's,' Dillon said to her. 'I have to get back – I have Maggie's car.'

'I want to go to my mother's,' Moira said, speaking not to him, but to the Inspector. 'She lives in Lurgan.'

'That's all right, we'll run you down there,' the Inspector said. 'If you want to take some things for the night, we'll make sure that everything's locked up here when we finish.'

'I don't need to take anything,' Moira said. 'I'll just get my coat.' She turned to Dillon. 'Will you come down to Mama's later on? I want to talk to you.'

'Yes, of course,' he said. He went to kiss her, but she walked out of the room. The Inspector watched her go, then turned to Dillon and asked quietly, 'You did see his face, did you?'

'Yes.'

'You could identify him, then?'

He nodded. 'Tell me,' he asked the Inspector. 'These people you were talking about, where did they go? The ends of the earth?'

The Inspector smiled. 'As a matter of fact, one man did go to Australia. But the other two cases I know of, the people just moved to England.'

'And they're all right?'

'So far, yes,' the Inspector said.

FOUR

A notice, hand-lettered on a sheet of white paper, had been thumbtacked below the main hotel entrance sign:

RESTAURANT CLOSED

BOMB DAMAGE

BAR OPEN   SANDWICHES

As he drove Maggie's car back through the security gates, he asked Billy if the Army bomb squad was still there.

'There's still soldiers here,' Billy said. 'But the bomb squad pulled out once the bomb went off. Bad luck about your car, eh, sir?'

'What about my car?'

'The wall collapsed on all them cars that was parked in the staff area. You'll see when you go in.'

He drove on. There was an Army barrier across the entrance to the car-park. He got out and went in on foot.

At first sight it seemed that the whole back part of the hotel had been destroyed, but as he walked across the car-park he saw that the damage was confined to the Emerald Room and the main dining-room adjoining it. The Emerald Room was a rubbled shambles, its outer wall completely collapsed, tables and chairs buried under falling brickwork, the ceiling hanging down like the broken wing of some huge prehistoric bird. The main dining-room was similarly destroyed. Where the outer wall had collapsed, his car and three others were completely invisible under rubble and bricks. From the almost total destruction of the cars it would, he realised, be difficult to tell in which one the bomb had been planted. As he walked closer to the wreckage, he saw a British Army armoured vehicle parked at the far end of the car-park and now a soldier with a rifle came up to him, waving him off.

'I'm the hotel manager,' he said. 'Tell me, were any of the bomb squad hurt?'

The soldier stared at him for a moment as if weighing up whether to answer, then said, 'No, sir. Sorry, you can't come any closer.'

'Thanks.' He nodded to the soldier and went out of the car-park. He looked at his watch. The university graduation ceremonies would be ending any time now. The graduates, their families and friends, would be coming here for lunch, drinks and celebrations. For most of them the first hint of anything wrong would be the sign *Restaurant Closed: Bomb Damage*. It would not stop them. Ignoring trouble was an Ulster tradition. Another wee bomb, as the local joke had it. By next week the whole incident would be forgotten.

'Michael?'

Coming towards him as he went up to the hotel's main entrance, was Rory Burke, his assistant manager. 'Where the hell were you?' Rory said. 'The big boss was on the phone from London, looking for you. He wants you to ring him right away. Are we open or not?'

'How bad is the damage?'

'Just what you saw back there. The kitchen's OK and, as far as we know, there's no structural damage elsewhere. Of course, the rooms on the floor above the restaurant – that whole corridor has been shut off.'

'Who put up that sign about the sandwiches?'

'Collis. We don't want to lose the bar business, do we? It's a big day, after all.'

'OK,' he said. 'Let's carry on. Business as usual. I'll check it with London, of course.'

'How did they get the bomb in?' Rory asked. 'Does anybody know?'

'No idea.'

'One of the police told Maggie it was probably a Semtex bomb, what they call a lunch-box bomb. I suppose anybody could have brought it in.'

'I suppose,' he said. 'Look, I'm going up to my office now to ring London. Would you give Maggie these keys to her car? Tell her it's OK to leave it where I parked it.'

He went ahead of Rory, going in at the front entrance but avoiding the reception area and using the service stairs to reach his office on the mezzanine. When he went into his office, he locked the door behind him. He dialled her number.

'Features,' a girl's voice said.

'Is Andrea there?'

'No, she just stepped away from her desk for a moment. Who will I say is calling?'

'Michael Dillon.'

'Just a minute.'

He waited. Then her voice. 'Are you all right? There was nobody hurt, was there?'

'No. It's all right.'

'God, what a day for you. You weren't there when it happened?'

'Yes, I was. I want to tell you about that.'

'I rang you half an hour ago,' she said. 'They couldn't find you. So I thought: He didn't come in. He's at home, telling Moira about us.'

Suddenly, he realised that, of course, she knew nothing.

'Listen,' he said. 'Could we see each other later today? This afternoon, maybe?'

There was a moment of silence. '*Did* you tell her?'

'Not yet.'

'I spoke to Somerville this morning,' she said. 'And he rang London and everyone's delighted, et cetera. Michael, you haven't changed your mind, have you?'

'Of course not. But something happened last night. I can't talk about it over the phone. Listen, can you meet me here this afternoon about three? And don't worry, I love you.'

Suddenly, the voice of one of the hotel operators cut in. 'Mr Dillon, I have London on the line. Mr Keogh's office. They said it's urgent.'

Had the operator heard him say, *I love you?*

'See you at three, then,' Andrea said. She hung up.

An Englishwoman's voice said, 'Is that Mr Dillon? Will you hold, please, for Mr Keogh?'

'Yes.'

With the Americans, the telephone had its protocols. The lesser person must always wait. Waiting, he thought of Keogh's office in Berkeley Square, the large conference rooms, the omnipresent computers, the waiting messengers, the fax machines, and, in Keogh's private office, two secretaries with calls on hold. It was a world of long-distance time zones, legal contracts, mergers, press conferences, grand openings, official receptions, double-parked limousines and, at its centre, Keogh, his tie loosened, phone cradled between shoulder and chin, calling back to his bosses in Los Angeles and New York, relaying reports on their hotels in London, Athens, Rome, Cannes, the smaller hotels in such places as Birmingham, Heraklion, Marseilles, and, this morning, Belfast, a recent minor acquisition which had not yet fully proven its worth.

'Michael,' said a familiar American voice, 'Dan Keogh. I hear you had a little action this morning?'

'Yes. We have some serious damage to the restaurant and one of the banqueting-rooms. But we're staying open. Is that all right? It's a big week – university graduations – and I don't want to lose the business.'

'Good thinking,' Keogh said. It was, Dillon knew, his favourite phrase. 'Reminds me of those old war movies,' Keogh said. 'Carrying on through the blitz. Listen, the reason I'm calling is, I'm sending Dwayne Harrison over to talk to you about clearing things up. He should be with you sometime this afternoon. As far as the Press is concerned, let's keep a low profile on the damage, OK? Any other problems?'

'Yes, well, if you have a minute, I have a personal problem. It's to do with what happened today.'

'Can you talk to Dwayne? Can he handle it?'

'Yes, I suppose so.'

'Good deal. You talk to Dwayne. I'm kind of tied up here at the moment. OK? Have a good day, Mike.'

Dismissed from Keogh's busy, money-breathing world, Dillon stood looking out at the mountain which reared up like a stage backdrop behind the city. Long ago, in school, daydreaming, he would look out of the classroom window and imagine himself in some aeroplane being lifted over that grey pig's back of mountain to places far from here, to London, New York, Paris, great cities he had seen in films and in photographs, cities far away from the dull constrictions of home. Outside now, in the mezzanine bar, familiar Ulster voices were raised in a wave of chat and jokes. It was as though he were still in that long-ago classroom, still daydreaming, still trapped.

His phone rang again. It could be Andrea. He picked it up.

'Mr Dillon, I have your father on line two.'

'Tell him I'm very busy. I'll call him later.'

The last person he wanted to speak to was his father. And he *was* busy. If Dwayne Harrison was arriving that afternoon he would expect damage reports, a contingency plan and all the rest of it. Again, the phone began to ring but this time he ignored it and went out of his office. People were coming up from the lobby, the graduation crowd mostly, but also a group of heating salesmen who had just finished a morning sales conference in the Dalriada Room. He moved downstairs to reception. Voices called to him: Was it the IRA, did anyone know? Was it the Army who blew the bomb up? When would he be able to open the restaurant again? The questions were, he knew, a way of expressing sympathy for him, a form of reassurance. No one had been hurt: there had been no atrocious deaths of people or animals. Just another bomb. Just an ordinary day, after all.

At reception, Rory Burke and Maggie were surrounded by anxious faces, groups whose graduation luncheons had been cancelled, guests whose rooms were in the damaged part of the hotel. There were also reporters, a photographer, a television crew. He joined Rory, answering questions, reassuring people, arranging to set up a cold buffet in the Craigavon Room. One of the waiters brought him hot coffee and toast which he ate while on the telephone to MacAnally, a contractor who had done the repair work in that earlier bombing. As the crowd swelled in the lobby and in the hotel's two bars, the noise, the questions, the chits to be signed, discussions with catering, the myriad details of the day, kept him from thinking of anything else. From time to time he would look at his watch and estimate how long it would be until Andrea came, but he did not think beyond that moment. He did not dare.

At about two o'clock with the bars still packed, the buffet food in the Craigavon Room ran out. As he went down the corridor to apologise to the long line of people who were still queuing up to be fed, a bellboy told him that Mr Harrison from London was waiting for him at the front desk.

Dillon checked his watch. He had not expected Harrison so early. 'Bring him up to my office, will you? I'll be there in a minute.'

Slowly, he went back up the stairs to his office. He had met Harrison before, two years ago, at a meeting of Alliance managers in London. Harrison was a Texan who had had his own accounting and business consulting firm before being brought in by Alliance to evaluate the performance and potential of the chain's assets. He was also known as the face you met when a hotel had to be closed or a manager fired.

When Dillon went into his office, Harrison was standing, a tall distant figure in a light-tan suit, looking out the window at an Army helicopter which was poised, stationary, over the nearby Catholic ghetto. He did not seem to hear Dillon come in. He stood, his hands clasped behind his back, rocking gently on his heels as he stared up at the sky.

'Hello, Dwayne,' Dillon said, speaking loudly over the helicopter noise.

Hesitantly, as though not sure his name had been called, Harrison looked over his shoulder at Dillon, then turned to greet him, throwing up his hands as if surprised. His pale chubby face, lips forever open in a half-smile, reminded Dillon of the face of a porcelain Victorian doll. 'Hey! How's it goin', man?' Dwayne said.

'I've had better days, as you can see.'

'True thing. Still, I guess this goes with the territory. Any idea why they picked us?'

'Yes. I want to talk to you about that.'

'OK, but let's look at the damage first. I've got to make the five o'clock shuttle back to London. I have a heavy meeting set up with some Italians tonight and it's too late to re-schedule it.'

'Let's go, then,' Dillon said. They took the lift down to the basement floor and at once Harrison went to work, taking notes on the damage, interviewing Collis on the catering problems, asking shrewd questions, taking down the name of the contractor Dillon was planning to hire for the repairs.

All the time Dillon's watch was inching closer to three, then passing three, and it was almost three-thirty when Sally, one of the reception clerks, came up to him. 'Excuse me, Mr Dillon, but there's a Miss Baxter waiting for you in the lounge.'

Harrison, behind him, asked, 'Urgent, Mike?'

'Sort of. If you can give me five minutes?'

'OK.' Harrison smiled his china-doll smile. 'I've got a couple of calls to make. See you back here.'

Almost hidden away behind the main reception lounge was a small room, a leftover from former times when it had been a writing room where guests caught up on their correspondence. Now, it contained a television set, some ugly black imitation-leather sofas and a soft-drink dispensing machine. As the bars and the main lounge also had television sets, it was the least used as well as the shabbiest room in the hotel. The television set was on, but the sound had been muted. As he went in he saw, peripherally, four contestants in a game show, sitting at false desks holding numbers above their heads. At once, Andrea, hidden from his view just inside the half-open door, came up to him and hugged him. She wore a T-shirt, jeans, running shoes and a military surplus combat jacket, all of it making her look about nineteen.

'I'm sorry,' she said.

'What are you sorry about?'

'I sounded mad at you on the phone, didn't I?'

'No, no. Look, I have to tell you about all that.'

She waited.

'We can't go to my office, damn it,' he said. 'I have to talk to you here.' He led her to one of the ugly sofas and sat down beside her. 'Listen. Last night, Moira and I had a visit from the IRA. The police have told me to say nothing about it to anyone. You'll see why, when I explain. I was the one who brought the bomb in here this morning.'

Beside Andrea, on the silent television set, a game show contestant held up a live mallard duck. A second contestant held up a duck decoy. From force of habit Dillon looked from time to time at the screen as he began, hurried, anxious, rushing his telling, telescoping the events of last night and this morning. She listened, her head nodding, saying small incoherent things to show her shock and sympathy. But, when he came to the part

87

where he went into the back room of the shop where the phone was, she turned to him suddenly and caught his arm, as though to prevent him from going on. 'You didn't phone?' she said, in a shocked voice.

'I had to. If I didn't phone I'd be an accomplice to those bastards. I'd be responsible for all those people being killed.'

'But what about Moira?'

'It's all right, it's all right,' he said. 'The IRA left our house before I telephoned. She's OK.'

'Oh, thank God,' Andrea said. 'Have you spoken to her?'

'Yes, I went home at once. But the police were there, we couldn't really talk. The police want us to leave the country, both of us.'

'Why's that?'

He did not answer because at that moment Rory Burke came into the room. 'Excuse me, Michael, his nibs is asking for you. I think he's getting a bit edgy.'

He stood up at once, saying to Andrea, 'Look, I have to go now. I've got this man from our head office in London and he's got to catch the five o'clock shuttle. Could you come back around five?'

'I don't know. I'll see.'

Rory said, 'You'll be along then, will you, Michael?'

'Yes. Coming.'

When Rory had gone out he held her and kissed her.

'What are you going to do?' she asked.

'It will be all right,' he said desperately. 'It will be all right. Five o'clock, OK?'

'I'm not sure about five. We're on the air at six. I'll try.'

'Anyway, I'll talk to you.'

'Go on, now, go on,' she said. And, when he was halfway through the doorway, she called, 'Michael? Take care.'

*

Dwayne Harrison, his long legs crossed, his hands gripping his right kneecap, sat in one of Dillon's office chairs, perfectly immobile, listening. When Dillon had finished telling his story Harrison got up and walked to the window. 'Well,' he said, in his slow Texan voice. 'This is a first, isn't it?'

'Sorry?'

'I mean this is some story, isn't it? It's the first time we've had to consider moving staff because hit men are after them. So, the cops want you to leave town?'

'Yes. They can't assign policemen to protect us. They seem to think that if we move to England we'll be a lot safer. As a matter of fact, I was planning to ask for a transfer soon. For personal reasons.'

Harrison threw his head back, laughed and slapped his thigh. 'Well, *this* is a personal reason, isn't it? But England's just next door. Would you be safe there?'

'I don't know if I'm going to be safe anywhere. But, safer than here, yes.'

'Mike, you've done a great job here. You know this territory better than anybody else. Who in hell are we going to get to replace you?'

'Rory Burke is bright.'

'He doesn't have your background,' Harrison said.

There was a silence and then Dillon said, 'What if I speak to Dan Keogh myself? What do you think? I was going to, in any case.'

Harrison stood up. '*I'll* speak to Dan,' he said. 'Look, this has been rough for you, we appreciate that. It's up to Dan, of course, but God damn it, if you hadn't made that phone call, we'd have had a real massacre on our hands. The way I see it, we owe you one. So, I'll speak to Dan and we'll get back to you tomorrow. Meantime, I don't have to tell you – take care. Now, can you get them to hustle me up a cab? I might just make the four-thirty shuttle if I'm lucky.'

When they went down, Jack, the doorman on duty, was waiting

for them at reception. He saluted. He had been told who Harrison was. 'Your taxi's here, sir.' He held up a large umbrella. 'I'm afraid it's a wee bit on the damp side out there.' He led them to the revolving doors, swinging the doors to let Harrison go in first. As Harrison entered the revolving doors a man was coming in from outside. When Dillon followed Harrison into the doors, the man, passing in the opposite direction, turned and stared at Dillon, as though he recognised him.

Outside, on the front steps, Jack opened the umbrella and guided Harrison to his waiting taxi. 'Call you tomorrow,' Harrison said as he eased his long body into the cab. Dillon waved and the taxi drove down towards the security gates which had been opened to let it exit.

At that moment, someone tapped him on the shoulder. 'Are you Mr Dillon?' said a male voice with a broad Belfast accent.

'Yes, what can I do for you?'

Facing him was the man who had seemed to recognise him a moment ago in the revolving doors. He was about forty with a broad white face, made larger by his domed, balding forehead. In the lapel of his shabby dark suit was a small enamel replica of a flag. The flag showed the Red Hand of Ulster in the centre, against a background of red-and-white stripes with the criss-cross pattern of the Union Jack. In his left hand he carried a dog-eared black leather-bound book.

'Could I have a word with you in private?' the man asked.

'What is it about?'

'Just a wee word with you. I won't keep you long. Is there somewhere we can go?'

They went back through the revolving doors and Dillon led him to the small unused television room where, earlier, he had been with Andrea. When they went into the room the man glanced back as if to make sure they were not being followed. He went over and turned off the image on the muted television set. 'If you don't mind,' he said, then looked back at Dillon. 'I'm here for Dr Pottinger.'

'Yes?'

'The police have told Dr Pottinger, in confidence, of course, about what you done here this morning. And Dr Pottinger has asked me to pass on to you his thanks for your courageous action. You're aware, of course, that this was an attempt on the Doctor's life?'

'Oh, was it?'

'Oh, there's no doubt about it. It was a deliberate attempt to murder him. I gather, then, from what your wife told the police, that neither one of you was aware of the purpose of the bomb?'

'That's right.'

'These IRA fellas never mentioned a word to either one of you all night?'

'No.'

'Funny, isn't it?' The man's white moonface slipped into a quick, guilty grin.

'Why is it funny? Why should they confide in us?'

The man hunched his shoulders, as though embarrassed.

'Is it because we're Catholics, is that what you mean?' Dillon said.

'Not at all, not at all,' the man said hastily. 'There's just one question we want to clear up. Inspector Randall says you and your wife don't want any mention made of your part in what happened. He says he advised you to stay out of this for fear of reprisals.'

'Yes, that's right.'

'And you're going to follow that advice?'

'Yes.'

'Good. So long as we know that. You see, Dr Pottinger is giving a press conference later on today and he wanted to be clear on that point.'

'I see.'

The man's fingers flipped the pages of the black leather-bound book absent-mindedly, as though considering what he must say next. The book was, Dillon saw, a Bible.

'Well, as I said, in that case Dr Pottinger will respect your decision.' Again the man's face creased in a grin. 'I gather you have no high opinion of the I R A, Mr Dillon?'

'No. Nor of Dr Pottinger either.'

The hand that held the Bible lifted it up as if making a debating point. 'Mr Dillon, we have many enemies. That is the penalty we pay for doing the Lord's work and speaking up for the people of Ulster. Thank you for your help. Have a good day.'

The man bobbed his head in farewell and, gripping his Bible, turned and left the room. Dillon stood, impotent in anger. What if Moira had been killed, would they still have had the nerve to come and thank me for what I'd done?

A bellboy's voice was paging him. 'Mr Dillon, please.'

He went out to reception. One of the bellboys came up, telling him there was a call for him. 'They said it was urgent,' the bellboy added. 'It's from the BBC.'

He ran upstairs to his office. The red light blinked on his phone. When he picked it up and said, 'Dillon here,' at once her voice, rushed, worried, speaking in a low tone as though she were in a place where she was overheard.

'Michael, I can't come at five. The taping's been pre-empted but I have to help out at a press conference. Funnily enough, it's about the bombing.'

'Is it Pottinger giving it?'

'Yes, how did you know?'

'Doesn't matter. When will you be free?'

'I don't know. I know we have to talk, but – '

'Listen,' he said. 'I have to drive down to Lurgan to see Moira. She's with her mother. She's going to stay there tonight. I'll tell her I have to come back here later. I'll make some excuse. Could we see each other at, say, ten?'

'At the hotel?'

'Yes. And listen. I spoke to Harrison just now. I think it's going to be all right about my transfer.'

'But what about Moira? You'll have to bring her, won't you?'

He was silent. 'Look, we'll talk about it. I'll see you at ten.'

'What a mess,' she said. 'It's a real mess, isn't it?'

'It will be all right,' he said desperately. 'Look, it will be all right.'

'How can it be?'

'Look, please – don't be upset. Andrea?'

There was silence on the line.

'Andrea?'

'Yes.'

'Listen, we'll talk about it. I'll work it out, it's going to be all right.'

'I'll see you at ten,' she said.

FIVE

The car which had been sent over from McAuley's, the car hire
people, was a small, shiny Fiat with less than five hundred miles
on the odometer. The motorway connecting Belfast with Lurgan
was well-designed and well-signposted, a high-speed autoroute
which provided occasional glimpses of new factories and neat
farmhouses set in well-tilled fields. It was a reminder that this
part of Ireland was a part of Great Britain, its roads and public
services far superior to those in the Irish Republic, less than a
hundred miles to the south. Driving on this road, Dillon might
be in one of the English shires. But tonight, he was reminded
of what, on a normal night, he would ignore. Visible on his right,
looking like a factory in the late summer's light, was the notorious
prison where, under British supervision, torture had been carried out, a place where Catholic and Protestant paramilitaries,
demanding to be treated as political prisoners, had refused to
wear prison garb, going about draped only in blankets, walking
their excrement-smeared cells like bearded Christs. It was a
place where the false martyrdom of IRA hunger strikers had
come to world attention, the prison the British called the Maze
and the Irish Long Kesh.

He looked at it now as he drove past. Men who had spent

years behind those walls were the organisers behind last night's nervous boys. Someone who might still be imprisoned there could have arranged for the Semtex bomb, the white Ford, the presence of a twelve-year-old delivery boy in the hotel car-park, the girl in the yellow muffler who followed him into the shop. This prison, which on a normal evening would be a familiar, ignored part of the landscape, had now become a factor in his life. He looked in the rear-view mirror at the cars moving in the lane behind him. Would one of them turn off with him, when the sign ahead said Craigavon? Which one would it be?

When he reached the turn-off and drove up the ramp to the roundabout which led to Lurgan, he pulled over to the side of the road and waited. But the only vehicle which followed him up the ramp was a bakery van which entered the roundabout then drove off in the opposite direction to the town. But what did that prove? They could be in that van. They had seen him pull over, and had moved on to deceive him.

He put the car in gear and drove on into the town, telling himself that he must stop thinking like this. Unless he did, from now on every suspicious-looking stranger, every innocent bakery van, would be an object of menace, a cause for alarm. But even as he warned himself he knew that he could not control it. He was afraid. He was not brave or defiant as he would have wished to be. He was afraid.

Moira's mother was a native of Lurgan. When Moira's father gave up his butcher's shop in Belfast, her mother had persuaded him to come back here and buy a house in the lower town. Dillon drove now into a street of row houses and small shops with, at its end, a railway station. The houses, built seventy years ago, had small cramped rooms, narrow back yards, and back windows opening on to an ugly rubbish dump. He drove around to the rear, and parked his car in a small lane on the edge of this dump.

As he went into her back yard, Moira's mother, standing by the kitchen window, saw him and came to the door to let him in. 'Michael, how are you?' she said, embracing him, pressing him against her large bosom.

'Hello, Maeve, is Moira here?'

'She is, surely. Come in, come in.'

Maeve was, Dillon sometimes thought, the unconscious first cause of Moira's bulimia. Like Moira she was tall, with beautiful hands and long elegant legs. But she had become fat, enormously fat, a corpulence emphasised by a relentless smoker's cough which made her gross body shake like a loose pudding. Unlike Moira she seemed blind to her surroundings so that the sitting-room into which she now ushered Dillon was as depressing as the lounge in an old people's home: plastic-covered sofa and chairs, a television set which was never shut off, garish kitsch paintings, cheap statuettes of nymphs and Disney animals, ethnic rugs and tasselled cushions, all of them purchased as souvenirs on package-tour holidays to the Costa Brava, Florida and the Algarve.

The room was empty. 'Where is she?' Dillon asked.

'She's upstairs, lying down,' Maeve said. 'Sure, she's whacked out. You must be the same, yourself. Could I get you a drink or something?'

At that moment he heard footsteps on the stairs outside and Moira's voice. 'Mama, is that Michael?' And then she came into the room. She did not greet him. 'I couldn't sleep,' she told her mother. 'And it's almost six. Will it be on the six o'clock news?'

It was. It was not the first item of news, which was a fatal airline crash in West Germany, nor the second which dealt with the resignation of a senior British Government adviser in a dispute with the Prime Minister. It was the third announcement. In even tones, the familiar BBC newsreader began, 'In Northern Ireland . . . ' and at once the screen was filled with television footage of the car-park, the wrecked cars and rubbled walls, the destroyed interiors of the restaurant and the Emerald Room. Dillon, sitting on the sofa with his mother-in-law, leaned forward, strangely excited. Suddenly, he had been plucked from the invisibility of ordinary life. There on television, watched by people all over the British Isles, were scenes and events he had helped to create. As the camera moved past the rubbled hotel wall into the debris of the Emerald Room, he heard the newsreader's voice say, 'The bomb was placed just outside this room in which the Reverend Alun Pottinger was speaking to a group of his supporters. While no group has yet claimed responsibility it is believed that this was an attempt to assassinate Dr Pottinger.' The image shifted to a half-dozen reporters and photographers surrounding Pottinger whose face, Dillon realised, looked more real on television than when he had seen it this morning.

'Dr Pottinger, do you think this was an attempt to assassinate you?'

'Ask the IRA. Of course it was. It would be a lot easier for the enemies of Ulster if I was out of the way.'

'Is this a change of tactics, then? There's never been an attempt to assassinate you before.'

Pottinger grinned into the camera. 'How do *you* know? Anyway I'm in good hands. God's hands. Thank you, now.'

The image shifted to the newsreader in the studio. 'In East London today . . . ' the newsreader began and at that point Moira got up and switched the set off.

Dillon turned and saw Moira's father Joe standing in the doorway, ruddy-faced, wearing his old bottle-green Barbour jacket, his Labrador tail-thumping behind him. 'Well, you're on the big news now,' Joe said, smiling. 'Hello there, Michael.'

'Hello, Joe.'

'I was just going to take the dog for his walk. I'll be back in a wee while.'

Joe went out again. 'Listen,' Maeve said. 'Have you had your supper?'

'No, not yet.'

'We'll have a bite here, then. You'll stay, won't you?'

'I will,' he said. 'Thanks.' Maeve went off to the kitchen.

Alone now with Moira, he turned, suddenly tense. She was sitting in one of Maeve's plastic-covered armchairs, her hands joined on her lap, looking out of the small window at a row of flowerpots which masked the ugly back yard from view. Clouds, heavy with rain, massed above the house.

'How are you?' he asked. 'How do you feel?'

She did not answer. She looked down at her feet, then, with her toe, eased her left sandal off until it dangled loose. She raised her long leg up, the sandal dangling, studying it as though waiting for it to fall on the floor.

'I came because you said you wanted to talk to me, remember?'

She eased the sandal back on to her foot. 'Are you afraid of them?'

'The IRA? Yes, in a way.'

'Are you going to run away?'

'I asked for a transfer today.'

'Without asking me?'

'It came up,' he said. 'I didn't have time. They sent Harrison over from London to see the damage. It just seemed logical to tell them what the police had told us.'

'I'm not going.'

If she did not come, if she did not want to come, then he would not be abandoning her, he would not have her like a millstone around his neck in London. 'What do you mean?' he said.

'I'm not leaving here. That's definite.'

'Why?'

'This is my country. I'm not going to let those bastards push me out of it.'

'But aren't you worried about being killed?'

'Yes, of course,' she said. He realised that she was not angry. The Moira who quickly lost her temper when you crossed her was not this woman who now looked at him as though he were a stranger she had met at a party, interested in his point of view, but willing to debate it.

'You'd be safer in London,' he said. 'At least, the police seem to think so.'

'But if we do leave,' she said, 'if people like us let the IRA push us around, how do you think we're ever going to change things?'

'I'm not here to change things.'

'That's true,' she said. 'This is a perfect excuse for you to run back to London.'

He wanted to say, It's up to you, but, at the same time, he was ashamed of wanting to say it. 'Look,' he said. 'I can't go to London and leave you here. What if something happens to you?'

'What if it does? Do you care?'

'What are you talking about?'

She walked across the small room and stood at the window, looking out at the gathering rainclouds. 'I think you know what I'm talking about.'

'Because I phoned the police? Is that it? Look, it's hard to explain. I know.'

'Do you know? *Do* you?' Her voice, calm until now, had a tiny tremor in it. She kept looking out the window. 'I sat at home and waited for you.'

He stared at her back. Was she crying?

'I didn't know what was happening to you,' she said. 'I didn't know about the bomb. I just knew they'd taken you away. They told me to stay in the room and not move, or you'd be killed. So, even when I heard them leave the house, I didn't move. I was afraid for you. Last night, when we were both in the house, I wasn't afraid of them. But this morning, knowing they had you, not knowing what they would do to you, I was no different from the poor bloody people who're so scared of them they keep their mouths shut when the police come around. I was afraid for you. But you weren't afraid for me, were you?'

She turned to look at him. She was crying.

'I was,' he said.

'No, you weren't. And the truth of it is you've never felt about me the way I do about you. And you never will. So go on, go to London. I'm staying here. Last night taught me a lesson. You can't avoid responsibility by pretending things aren't there.'

'What do you mean?'

'Oh, come on,' she said. 'You know what I mean. You and me.'

'Listen – ' he said.

'No, you listen. You stood up to them this morning. You were willing to lose me to do it. Well, I'm going to stay here now and stand up to them, even if it means losing you.' She turned away. 'What am I talking about? I can't lose you. I never had you.' Again, she began to cry. At that moment, he heard the sound of the front door opening. 'Give me a Kleenex,' she said. He gave her one and she wiped her eyes hurriedly as her father came into the front hall.

'Come on, Rex, come on,' her father said, pulling at the old dog's lead, dragging him into the hall. 'It's started to rain,' her father said. 'We had to come back. But he doesn't want to come back, poor old fella. He misses his walk.'

'Is that Dada?' Maeve's voice called from the kitchen.

'It is,' Joe said.

'Good thing you came home. Supper's ready.'

In a small alcove off the kitchen, the table was laid with plates of ham and a lettuce-and-tomato salad, a loaf of soda bread, a teapot and cups. Rex, thumping his tail against the table leg, settled in under the white tablecloth, snug at his master's feet. Dillon saw that, as usual when he and Moira ate with her parents, her mother had set out her best china and silver and at each place a freshly ironed linen napkin replaced the paper ones she would normally use. He knew this was done because Moira had laid down the rules. For she was, at once, her parents' devoted daughter and their judge. Her schooling with the Sacred Heart nuns had erased her broad Belfast accent, so that she did not speak like a girl who was their child. Her university degree, the first ever earned on either side of her family, and, above all, her marriage to Dillon who had been born of parents who made hers feel ill-at-ease, all of it had changed Joe and Maeve's roles, so that now it was as though they were Moira's children, warned to sit up straight, to mind their table manners and be on their best behaviour when she put them on public view. And even tonight, after knowing what had happened in the past twenty-four hours, that awkwardness persisted in the way they poured the tea, passed the soda bread and offered more ham as soon as Dillon began to finish what was on his plate.

It was then that he noticed Moira had eaten nothing except a slice of tomato and some lettuce. It was a bad sign. He wondered if she had seen chocolates somewhere in the house. Or would she go out to get them later, under pretence of taking a walk?

He looked at the window. Rain blurred the windowpanes. Joe was talking, quietly at first, asking questions about last night. But then he put his napkin down on the table and in a way Dillon had never heard him speak before said, 'My daughter! *My daughter!* Sittin' in her house with the IRA pointin' a gun at her head. Before the war, when I was a wee boy, if anyone had told me that, I'd have said you're daft. I mean, back then the IRA was finished, a bunch of dodos that nobody heeded any more. Sure, we had the same Troubles in those days, a Catholic would never get a job if there was a Protestant up for it. But then the war came and there was more jobs and I used to think all that bigotry's dyin' out and after the war things will get better. But they didn't. And then in the sixties the civil rights marches started and it was on the telly an' the whole world saw the Prods beatin' us up and the police helpin' them. And I thought: Now that the outside world sees what's goin' on here, things will get better. But they got worse. And you know the rest. After all this fightin' there's more Catholic unemployed here than ever there was. And we're being "protected" by the IRA, a bunch of thugs, that has no programme except killin' people. They're against the Irish Government as much as they're against the Brits. And who are they for? Themselves! And who's for them? Nobody, except some stupid Yanks who know nothin' about what's goin' on here, and a few of my people, people born in the Falls Road and places like that. And the worst of it is, it's people like us, ordinary Catholics, who are the only ones who can stop them. Instead of that we're helpin' them to go on destroyin' this country because we're too stupid to see the truth. And too frightened of them gettin' back at us.'

He stopped abruptly and coughed as though he were weeping and trying to hide it. Then he laughed, embarrassed. 'Soap-box speech,' he said. 'Sorry about that.'

Moira's hand reached across the table to grip her father's sleeve. 'You're right, Dada, you're dead right. Listen, I just told Michael. I'm not running off to England. I'm not going to let them dictate my life.'

'Now, wait a minute,' Maeve said. 'What is this? Another martyr for the cause? You'd stay here and get yourself killed to make a political point against the IRA. Is that what I'm hearing? Is it? Because, if it is, it's a lot of nonsense. You'd be getting killed for nothing. I'm as Irish as anybody, but I can't see that any of this is worth dying for. Getting rid of the IRA? Getting a fair shake for Catholics in jobs and at the polls? A united Ireland? Have some sense. The South of Ireland doesn't want us and couldn't take care of us if we were handed to them on a plate tomorrow. It's all madness, this, madness, and don't you be going and getting mixed up in it.'

'Did you hear what Dada said?' Moira turned angrily on her mother. 'It's people like us who're the only ones who can stop them. And we're not going to stop them by letting them run our lives. Do you know what I should do? I should tell the whole world what happened to us last night. I should tell the way they treated us. I should come out into the open and say this is what happened. My husband had to choose between saving his wife's life or saving the life of the likes of Pottinger. We should stand our ground. And then, if we're shot, the whole world will know why we're being shot. And I don't think even the most stupid of the people who back the IRA would say that it was fair.'

'You'd be surprised,' her father said wearily. 'Who's talkin' about bein' fair? The people who back them are used to shuttin' their eyes to things they don't want to see. If the pair of you are killed, it will just be a warnin' to the rest of the people who's afraid of them.'

'Would you listen to yourself?' Moira said. 'Aren't you the one who said, a minute ago, that we're the only people who can stop them? Well, when are we going to start?'

Her father stared at her across the table with sad, shamed eyes. 'It's all very well for me to talk,' he said. 'But you're my daughter. You're what matters.'

'That's right,' Maeve cut in. 'Now you're talking sense.' She turned to Michael. 'Michael, you haven't said a word. What do you think?'

'What does he think? It's no use asking him,' Moira burst out angrily. 'First thing today, he asked for a transfer to London. Didn't bother consulting me. What does *he* think? He never wanted to come back here, he's been waiting for the day he can get out of Northern Ireland for ever. This is a godsend for him. Isn't it?'

She turned, staring at him.

'Yes,' he said. 'I left here a long time ago. It wasn't my choice to come back. Now, I never want to see this place again.'

There was a silence in the room, a silence broken only by the dog who rose up beneath his master's feet and poked his snout out from under the tablecloth between Moira and Dillon, turning this way and that, silently begging for a scrap of food. Dillon put his hand on the dog's head, fondling him.

At last, Maeve said, 'Well, in a way I can't blame you, Michael. But, listen, we don't want any rows here tonight. You're both dead tired. Michael, you'll stay the night, won't you?'

'I'm sorry,' he said. 'I have things to do at the hotel. I'll sleep there.'

When he said that, Moira pointedly looked out the window. 'Do you think the rain's over?' she asked her father.

'It was just a shower.'

'All right, then. I'll take Rex for his walk.'

'I can do it. You stay here,' her father said.

'I *want* to.' She stood up. 'Here, Rex,' she called, and went out of the dining-room with the dog galumphing behind her. Her parents sat listening, as though waiting for her to leave.

When they heard the front door close, Maeve asked, 'How has she been, Michael? Has she been all right?'

He shrugged as if to say he was not sure.

'She's all right,' Joe said. 'She's a great wee girl. She has more spirit than the rest of us, that's all.'

'Don't you be encouraging her, do you hear?' Maeve said angrily. She turned to Dillon. 'You wouldn't leave without her, would you?' And then, as if ashamed of having said it, she put her hand on his and gave it a small squeeze. 'Sorry. Of course not. Not to worry. Her father and I will speak to her.'

'She's just high strung,' Joe said.

SIX

He waited for almost an hour, but Moira did not come back to the house. Was she sitting in some field gorging chocolates? Or, more likely, was she walking in Lurgan Park, the dog weary behind her as she covered mile after mile, hurrying as if to catch a train? Her angers were like fevers. She fought them alone: running out of the house, sometimes taking the car, sometimes on foot, but always wandering restlessly, aimlessly, until her rage fell, like mercury in a thermometer. Then, silent, almost furtive, she would come home, avoiding him, going to sleep in the spare room, alone.

At nine when she had not returned, he said goodbye to Maeve and Joe. As he approached the roundabout which led to the motorway he noticed two cars following him. He pulled his car over, waiting to see if they slowed down. But they blazed past him and, when he came on to the motorway and turned in the direction of Belfast, there were no vehicles in sight.

Twenty minutes later he arrived at the hotel. When he parked his car at the side entrance, crowds of celebrating students, many with drinks in hand, were wandering about in the fenced-off car-park inside. Floodlights, installed last year as a security measure, lit up the bomb damage, the rubble, the gaping walls, the sagging ceilings, like some macabre *son et lumière* spectacle. Inside the hotel, both bars were full. Groups of young people stood drinking in the lobby as though at some gigantic cocktail party. When he went past reception he saw that Collis had transformed the ballroom into an impromptu dining area and had put up a sign offering a *prix fixe* buffet 'For Hotel Guests Only'. But there were three times as many people being fed there as there were guests in the hotel.

In his office a dozen telephone message slips lay scattered on his desk. He sifted through them to see if Andrea had called. His father had rung twice, other friends, fellow hotel managers. And there was a message from Keogh's secretary. *Mr Keogh will call you tomorrow at nine.*

That will be my answer; Harrison has told him. One way or another, he has made up his mind.

He rang down to reception. 'Michael Dillon. Listen, I have to spend the night. Do we have any rooms at all?'

'We're full up, Michael. With those rooms being damaged over the restaurant, we had to do a bit of reshuffling. And, of course, we were busy to begin with. Oh, wait – ' She laughed. 'There's the Jacuzzi.'

The Jacuzzi was the staff's private name for the most expensive suite in the hotel. It had been planned as a penthouse suite by the American decorator who had redone the Clarence, but even when Dillon offered it at a discount it was hard to rent: its appointments and price were still too rich for local tastes.

'The Jacuzzi, then,' he said. 'I don't mind roughing it.'

'I'll check with the housekeeper and see that it's made up for you.'

'Thanks, Sheila,' he said. He put the phone down. Suddenly, feeling he was being watched, he turned in his chair. Framed in the doorway of his office, staring at him fixedly, was a tall boy, his dark greasy hair long about his collar, his face deathly pale and wet with sweat, his eyes glazed as though on drugs. He wore a black T-shirt, jeans and dirty running shoes. His hands were deep in the pockets of an oversize leather windbreaker. Dillon looked again at the jeans and the running shoes. The tall youth from last night?

'Yes?' Dillon said.

The boy's hand shifted suddenly in the deep pocket of his windbreaker. The pocket was large enough to hide a gun. Like an animal transfixed in a hunter's sights, Dillon sat utterly still. The boy stared at him, sweating, silent. The boy's eyes dilated. He opened his mouth as if to scream or shout, but no sound came. Then, in panic, he turned and bolted down the corridor. Dillon stood up shakily, and went to the door. He saw the boy stop, halfway down the corridor. Was he coming back? Quickly, Dillon caught the door, to close it, but as he did the boy leaned his head against the corridor wall and, bending over, retched. A stream of yellow vomit splashed on the carpet. Dillon stood, staring, as the boy wiped his mouth and went unsteadily towards the staircase. A frightened assassin? No, of course, of course, a drunk boy up here, looking for the men's room. The corridor was empty now, the vomit a small smelly pool on the floor. He went back into his office and sat down. Fear, and the sight of the vomiting boy, had made him physically ill. A wave of nausea came and passed. From the mezzanine he heard the loud dull roar of bar talk, punctuated by occasional bursts of laughter. It was as though he listened to voices from another world. In that world, last night, walking on the Lagan towpath, he had been filled with plans, free to make choices, a man in control of his life. Again, from the mezzanine, he heard the roar of talk, the shouts of student laughter. Here, in this room, sick with fear, it was as though he had left that world for ever.

The phone rang. He looked at the panel and saw it was a house line. When he picked up the receiver, her voice, different from any other, said, 'It's me, will I come up?'

'Yes. I'll meet you at the stairs.'

He went out along the corridor, past the small pool of vomit, saw her coming up the winding staircase, met her, held her and kissed her.

'Where will we go?'

'Wait,' he said. 'I have to get a key.'

A few minutes later, on the top floor of the hotel, he unlocked the door of the penthouse suite. Andrea walked through the sitting-room with its large sofa, swivel armchairs and outsize television set. She went into the bathroom, saw the jacuzzi, then went into the bedroom with its large circular bed. When she saw the bed she turned and looked at him. 'What on earth?' she said, and laughed.

'It was the Yanks' idea. They didn't realise they were dealing with a Third World country.'

Far below in the grounds of the hotel voices began to chant a song. With Andrea, he went to the sitting-room window and looked down. Crowds of celebrating students had spilled out of the lobby into the front-entrance yard and now, under the security floodlights, they linked arms, singing and cavorting like actors on a stage. Andrea looked down at them, happy, young, drunk, then turned and looked at him. 'Oh, God. What are we going to do?'

'It's all right,' he said. 'It's going to be all right.'

'How can it be?' she said. 'Last night when you said you'd come with me to London I was happier than I'd ever been in my life. And then you went home and this happened.'

'Wait,' he said. 'Let's have a drink.' He went to the minibar and took out two little whisky bottles. 'Can you stay the night?'

'Yes.'

They sat down on the sofa. He poured her whisky and she drank it down as though it were medicine. 'What are you going to do?' she asked.

'Keogh, my boss, is going to ring here in the morning. My guess is he's going to transfer me. Do you still want to go to London with me?'

'What are you talking about? What about Moira? You can't leave her now, can you?'

'She says she's not going to go. She's making a crusade of it.'

'Why?'

'It's too long to explain but she's serious. She knows I'm going. I haven't told her about you yet, but I will. I mean, if you still want to be with me.'

'Why wouldn't I?'

'The IRA – all that. It could be dangerous, being with me.'

She laughed shakily. 'But I always knew that,' she said. Then, serious, she asked, 'Do the police think they'd follow you over there?'

'They didn't say. But they did imply it would be more dangerous if I stayed here.'

'Then it could be dangerous right now. Right this minute.'

'Maybe you'd better not stay the night.'

She laughed. 'You're not getting rid of me that easily,' she said, standing up and walking back into the bedroom. He followed her in. 'Can you believe this bed?' she said.

'Can we live up to it?' he said.

She smiled and pulled down the zip of his trousers. And, at once, it was as if his fear was transformed into an urgent, driving lust. She was unbuttoning his shirt as he unhooked her skirt and pulled down her panties. Naked, she ran around the big circular bed, then, lifting back the ornate coverlet, she jumped up on the bed like a child, using it as a trampoline. He stood, naked, watching her slim, almost boyish body shooting up and down like a diver on a springboard, her hair swirling loose about her shoulders, as, jumping, she slowly turned to face him. Now, he saw the small dark circle of pubic hair on her flat athlete's stomach. The room seemed to shake with her movements; the bed creaked under its punishment. It was as though she were on a stage, acting out some joyous festive rite while he stood, looking up, a spectator, seeing that world of spontaneous gaiety from which he was now shut out.

And, in that moment, as though she sensed his changed mood, she collapsed in the centre of the great circle of bed and, lying full length on her stomach, looked at him. 'What's wrong?'

He could not speak. He sat on the bed, stroking her back, his hand moving up and down over the arch of her buttocks until, rolling over, she pulled him down on her, straining her naked body against his as though she would fold them into one person. And then, reunited, they entered that eclipse of time, the act of making love.

Later, while she slept, he lay looking at her in the reflected yellow glare of the security floodlights which were trained on the hotel grounds. She was not, like Moira, a beauty who drew instant male attention. When he thought of her he did not, at once, see her face. Was this, he wondered now, a different kind of love? With Moira it had been the love of her looks, pride in the temporary possession of someone other men admired, an obsession which thrived on the danger of being displaced by another, more attractive male. His love for Moira, he now knew, had not been love but a form of self-deceit. He had not tried to dispel her fears or to know and help that angry, sentimental, discontented girl who used the sword of her beauty to assure her the indulgence of the men with whom she dealt.

And what did he know of Andrea? He did not think of her looks but of the feeling he had that the hours he spent with her were the hours that mattered most in his life. It was a happiness he did not risk by any attempt to define it, a happiness which made him lonely each time she left him. She was more open, more honest, than any other girl he had known. She seemed to have no hidden fears. Yet did he really know her any better than he had known Moira? Who is Andrea, what is she? What is she dreaming now?

She stirred in her sleep. Her hand, small and plain, the nails cut short, twitched as her fingers plucked at the sheet. What if she, not Moira, had been with him last night? Would she have jumped recklessly from the bathroom window, would she have stood up to them, risking their anger? Or would they have seemed to her, as they never would to Moira, dangerous unknowns like airline hijackers who must be placated and obeyed but who, if one survived the hijack, would disappear from one's life like figures in a bad dream? Of course they would. They were no part of Andrea's life. Was he being selfish in involving her in all of this? If he really loved her he should stay away from her now. But he could not. He did not have the courage to risk losing her.

Shortly after dawn they woke and made love. The yellow search-lights had been turned off outside and the pale morning sky was the colour of milk. Gulls wheeled and called in the early silence as, lying in each other's arms, they heard the city waken, the heavy rumble of long-distance trucks moving towards the motorway, the distant thunder of a plane. At seven she lay in the jacuzzi, laughing as he fumbled with the various faucets. Then, holding her, her back against his chest, his hands on her breasts as the faucets bubbled on their bodies, his mood soared. Suddenly, it was as if he was already away from Belfast, away from Moira, living in a new and permanent state of happiness. But at eight, when, bathed and dressed, they prepared to leave the room, reality closed in.

'We'd better not have breakfast here,' she said. 'What do you think?'

'We could go down the road, I suppose. There's a place called the Bewley. But, wait, what's it matter now? I'll have to tell her today.'

When he said that, she reached up and kissed him. 'Still,' she said. 'I think it would be easier if we go out somewhere. The staff here would see us having breakfast. They know you spent the night here. Gossip. All that.'

'You're right. Let's go out.'

'I'll go down now and wait for you in the lobby,' she said. 'It's not far, this place, is it? We can walk?'

'It's five minutes away.'

He let her out. When she had gone down the corridor to the lift, his room phone rang. It could be my father, he's been ringing since yesterday. He let the phone ring and, when it stopped ringing, he went out, locking the door. The corridor was empty. She had already gone down.

When the lift came, he saw inside it Ernie, one of the porters, with a loaded baggage trolley. This was something that was forbidden. Porters were supposed to take the service lift unless a guest accompanied the baggage. Ernie, guilty, said, 'Morning, sir,' then avoided his eye, hoping not to be challenged on his fault. At the third floor two guests got on and when the lift reached the lobby Ernie held the door open, nodding to him again as he followed the guests out.

As he crossed the lobby, Duffy, the night manager, waved to him from the reception desk. 'You're in early,' Duffy said.

'I slept here. I'm going out for a minute. Back soon.'

He saw her, standing by the news-stand. She had bought two newspapers and was reading one of them. As he went towards her he saw that the clock over the stand showed eight-fifteen. And remembered: Keogh was to call at nine, but might call before then.

'All right?' she asked.

'No. Sorry, but we've got to eat here. I forgot. I'm expecting that call from London.'

She hesitated, and then, in the sudden way she had, she laughed, said, 'What the hell,' and walked ahead of him into the dining-room.

The dining-room area which was normally used for breakfasts had been diminished by half because of the bombing. Now, only ten tables were set, closed off by banquet screens. Luckily, all of the tables were not yet taken. Alice, the hostess who came up to him, smiled and shrugged. 'A wee bit cramped, aren't we?' she said.

'Can we have that table?'

'Certainly, Mr Dillon.' She seated them and waved menus in the air. 'No sense handing out these. We don't have a full breakfast on. All we can do is juice, coffee and toast. We might manage boiled eggs. Would you like boiled eggs, Miss?'

'No, thanks. Orange juice and toast,' Andrea said.

He remembered then about the phone call. 'Excuse me,' he said. He went into the lobby, picked up a house phone and told the switchboard where he was.

When he came back she was reading the newspaper. 'Listen to this, Michael. There's a story here about the bomb. They're saying that, if it was an attempt to murder Pottinger, then it's a whole new change of policy for the IRA because until now they've never targeted him. They point out that if the bomb had gone off with no warning it would have killed hundreds of people besides Pottinger. The police say the IRA didn't give any warning but they won't say how they found out about it.' She looked at him. 'That means they're trying to protect you, aren't they?'

'Yes.'

'But what's the point? The IRA must know that it could only have been you who told.'

'Or Moira,' he said. 'They left before the bomb was due to go off. She could have been the one who phoned the police.'

'Oh, God. I didn't think of that.'

The waitress had arrived with coffee and their breakfasts. 'Will there be anything else?' the waitress asked.

He shook his head. Andrea sat, not looking at him, staring at her coffee cup. 'So you're in equal danger?' she said.

'Yes, I suppose.'

'If you go to London with me and she stays here and something happens to her – you know what I'm thinking – how would we feel?'

'I don't think anything's really going to happen.' He said it angrily, frightened that if Andrea thought about it she might change her mind.

'But you can't be sure, can you? She really should go, shouldn't she? And if you tell her about us it gives her another good reason not to go.'

'Look, it's up to her. It has nothing to do with me any more.' But even as he spoke he knew he had said something ignoble, something Andrea might remember and hold against him. Now, trying to correct his mistake, he said, 'And if I do go along with her stupid notion and stay here, and you leave and I lose you? Look, it was over between Moira and me before this ever happened. She's not going to go, no matter what I do, no matter what I say. I know her.'

She did not speak. She sat, looking at him, as though she were trying to make up her mind. At nearby tables, conversations continued in the churchly tones which people adopt when in a public place. Beyond the screens a plastic sheet had been erected over the gaping hole in the restaurant wall and, in the car-park outside, he could hear the contractor's trucks arriving to start work on rebuilding. The whispered voices, the background noise of the trucks, made her silence even more threatening. Then, at last, she reached her hand across the table and said, 'All right. If you're sure?'

He put his hand on hers. 'I'm sure.' As he did he glanced at the tables near by. No one was looking at them. And then, coming towards him from the dining-room entrance, he saw Alice, the breakfast hostess. Behind her, tall, walking quickly, was Moira.

'Now, Mrs Dillon,' Alice said, waving Moira on, pointing to his table, then turning, with a professional smile, to return to her station. Moira came up to him. She was wearing the same red shirtwaist dress she had worn last night, her feet in sandals, walking with that quick lithe swing of her hips as though she were a model in a fashion parade.

He stood up. Did she see us? 'Hello there,' he said to her, trying to keep his voice casual and easy. He turned to Andrea. 'This is my wife, Moira. Moira, this is Miss Baxter of the BBC.' He pulled out a chair. 'Have you had breakfast?'

'Yes,' Moira said. She did not sit down. 'I was just on my way home.' She looked at Andrea. 'Would you excuse us for a minute?'

'Yes, of course,' Andrea said. She stared up at Moira.

'Won't be long,' he said. Moira nodded to him, indicating that they should go out in the lobby. Had she seen them, would she make a scene, would he tell her now?

When they reached the lobby, Moira looked back into the dining-room. 'Who's that girl?'

'I told you. She works for the BBC. What was it you wanted to see me about?'

She looked at him and suddenly, watching the skin around her cheekbones tighten as though she would scream, he knew she had seen them holding hands. 'I just stopped off on my way into town,' she said. 'I wanted to tell you. You remember what we were talking about last night?'

'At supper, yes.'

'Well, I've been thinking about it all night. I mean it. Go to London if you want. But I'm definitely staying here.'

It was the moment to tell her, but he knew he could not do it. Not with Andrea so close. 'We'll talk about it later,' he said. 'Will you be home this afternoon?'

'No. I rang Peg Wilton this morning. I'm starting right away in her shop. How long have you known that girl?'

'What girl?'

She jerked her head in the direction of the dining-room. '*That* girl!'

'A few months. Why?'

Suddenly, she laughed, angry, close to hysteria. 'Why?' she said. '*Why?*'

At that moment, Jimmy, one of the bellboys, came running across the lobby. 'Mr Dillon, you're wanted on the phone. They said it's London.'

'That's my boss,' he told Moira. 'It's about the transfer.'

She looked at him. For a moment he thought she was going to hit him, but she said, 'Go on, then. I have to go myself,' and walked back across the lobby with her swift angry stride.

He watched her as she pushed her way through the revolving doors. He then signalled Jimmy and pointed to Andrea's table. 'Tell that lady I'll be back in a moment. Tell her it's London on the line.' He ran towards the mezzanine stairs and his office.

As always, Keogh's secretary made sure he was standing by before transferring the call to her boss. He waited, tense, until the familiar voice said, 'Hi, Mike. Dan Keogh. How's it going?'

'Fine.'

'Mike, I've been talking to Dwayne and we're going to pull you out. You worked at the Ormonde didn't you?'

'Yes, years ago.'

'I'm going to put you back in there. As an assistant manager. How does that grab you?'

'Terrific. Thank you.'

'OK, come on over as soon as you can pack up. Hold it – '

He waited on a silent line until Keogh's voice came back on again. 'Mike, I got to hang up on you. Burke – that the name of your assistant?'

'Yes.'

'Tell him to take over but don't raise his hopes. OK? Dwayne's looking for a replacement for you there. Bye, Mike. See you soon.'

'Thanks,' he said again, but Keogh had already rung off.

The Ormonde, one of the grander hotels in the Alliance chain, looked out, like the Grosvenor and the Dorchester, on to a view of Hyde Park. He had worked there for six months while in training and had heard a rumour that the Ormonde's manager, Ronny Pomfret, was a year or two away from retirement. Dillon stood, looking out at bleak Belfast rooftops, but seeing the long sweep of the Ormonde's façade, the waiting queue of London taxis under the *porte-cochère*, the top-hatted doormen escorting veiled Arab ladies and their attendants towards waiting limousines. He remembered calm lobbies filled with flowers and the baskets of fruit and buckets of champagne sent up with compliments to the suites of important guests. He thought of the smooth patina of Ronny Pomfret's days, the Jaguar waiting in the hotel's underground garage to drive him home to his villa in the stockbroker belt, his children in good schools, his holiday house in Provence. If Keogh is putting me in now as an assistant manager, there's always the chance . . .

But then, like a referee's whistle signalling a foul, a police siren sounded outside. Suddenly, in clear focus, he saw again the Belfast rooftops, the grey mountain looming over the city. Even his momentary daydream seemed tawdry, for wasn't it a proof that his ambition in life had shrunk to a vision of himself as a head flunkey in morning clothes, a glorified servant, condemned to smile and turn the other cheek to the condescension, bad manners and arrogant assumptions of people who could pay hundreds of pounds for a night's lodgings? And Andrea? Would she be content to live with such a man and for how long?

At the thought of Andrea he hurried back down to the lobby. She was coming out of the dining-room. 'Has she gone?' she asked.

'Moira? Yes.'

'What happened?'

'Nothing, really. I was called to the phone and she left. Listen, the transfer's OK. That was London on the line.'

When he said that, Andrea looked at him in a way that worried him. 'I have to run,' she said. 'I'll talk to you later.'

'Look.' Alarmed, he took hold of her wrist. 'It *is* all right, isn't it?'

'I hope so,' she said, and pulled herself free. 'Bye, Michael.'
She walked quickly across the lobby and, as Moira had minutes
before, pushed through the revolving doors and was gone.

SEVEN

Inset in the heavy front door were two leaded panels of coloured glass: circles, triangles, and squares of pink, yellow and green which gave a distorted, drunken view into the front hall. When he turned the key and pushed open the door the movement sent the post scattering across the shiny linoleum within. The morning newspaper was stuck halfway through the letterbox. He did not bother to remove it. He closed the door behind him and stood in the kaleidoscopic shadows cast by the coloured glass. The house was quiet as a church. There was no sign that the police had been here. He looked in at the open doorway of the sitting-room. The sofa, the television set, the chairs, no longer looked familiar. It was as though he had left this house, not yesterday, but years ago, and now, coming back into it again, he saw it as a stranger would, shabby, ordinary, with pictures and ornaments which, were he the owner, he would at once remove.

In the kitchen, the alarm clock on the dresser ticked loud as a metronome. The formica-covered table and four kitchen chairs seemed odd and unfamiliar. Was it here that four men in woollen balaclava helmets sat waiting for morning and a bomb to go off? He turned and went back into the hall. He climbed the stairs.

Is this the house where Moira and I lived three years as man and wife? How strange it seems, a house rented for a summer month at the seaside, a place I will drive past a year from now, wondering which front door was mine.

On the landing he looked in at the bedroom, at the unmade bed, at Moira's blue nightgown lying on it, rucked up from where the tall IRA youth had sat. He opened the wardrobe. His clothes, on racks and shelves, seemed like everything else here, as though they belonged to someone else. He found a suitcase, and began tossing clothes into it. Minutes later, in the room which had been his study, he took from a drawer the documents and papers he had set aside the other night. As he closed the drawer he looked at the wall of books, those books which were the only things here he had felt to be his own. Were there some he should take now? For he sensed he would never see them again.

He went to the window and looked out at the avenue. Between the hours of ten a.m. and four p.m. the avenue was usually empty of traffic other than delivery vans and service vehicles. Now he saw, coming towards him, a white Ford car. The Ford seemed the same one which had kept him under surveillance the night before last. It drove slowly past his house and, as it did, he saw the top of the driver's head, and his hand, loosely gripping the wheel. The Ford drove on up the avenue, stopped at the intersection, then turned right and disappeared.

Was it the same Ford? Should he telephone the police? Or would he seem hysterical, a fool? White Ford cars were common. It was a coincidence, that's all.

He told himself to calm down. He put the papers he had come for in his suitcase and shut the case. He walked slowly downstairs to the front hall and stood, listening for the sound of the white Ford coming back. He heard only the loud tick of the kitchen clock. They had probably seen him drive up and now they would be watching for him to come out, get into his car and drive off. The white Ford would follow him.

Leave the car. Don't go near it. Go out the back way.

He went down the hall and opened the back door which led into the garden. He looked right and left at the other gardens in the entryway. There was no one in sight. He shut the door and ran up the garden path to the gate. When he reached the gate he saw ants, marching in a column across the path, to and fro from Teddy's blood-clotted body. Suddenly, it seemed more dangerous to go out this way. If they were watching the front they would also watch the back. Walking alone up the entryway and into the avenue he would be a clear target. He turned, and ran back into the house. He went down the hall and opened the front door. The avenue was deserted except for a small boy, riding his tricycle on the pavement. He went out the front door and ran down to the street, throwing his suitcase into the back seat of the car. He put the car in gear and drove down the avenue watching for the white Ford. He came on to the main road, meeting a stream of traffic. There was no white Ford in sight.

Peg Wilton's antique shop was in the centre of the city in an area forbidden to motor traffic. At the gates of this enclave, security guards carried out perfunctory searches of the hand baggage of pedestrians entering the area. Apart from this precaution it could have been a prosperous shopping area in any British city. Department stores, clothing boutiques, restaurants and furniture showrooms were crowded in the mid-morning shopping rush. There were no signs of bomb damage in these central streets, no graffiti, no armed police or British Army patrols. Peg's place was beside a large toyshop whose windows were alive with electronic games and wind-up toy cars and trucks which bumped into obstacles, overturned, righted themselves, and continued their meaningless progress. A group of children stood, intent as military observers, watching these displays as Dillon passed by and went in at Peg's door to the sound of a shop bell. The shop seemed to specialise in old costume jewellery, silver photograph frames, Tiffany-style lamps and antique mirrors. It was empty of customers. As he entered, Peg appeared from a little room in the back. She wore a flowered yellow silk dress and carried, affectedly, a long silver cigarette holder in which there smouldered a half-smoked cigarette.

'Michael!' She embraced him, touching her velvet cushion cheek against his, left, then right, like a French general bestowing a military honour. 'I heard!' she said. 'Isn't it awful – and unbelievable? To think I was in your house earlier that same night!'

'Where's Moira, is she here?'

'Moira, my dear, has just been seen on Ulster Television. Didn't you know?'

'No. What about?'

'Well, she's decided to tell exactly what happened to both of you that evening. I think it's really brave of her, don't you?'

'How did she get on the telly so soon?'

'When she told me the story this morning she asked if I knew anyone from the papers who would listen to her and, of course, I'm a great friend of Penny Davis, you know, *The Morning Show*, so I rang Penny up. And, of course, it was a scoop for Penny. They rushed her over to the studios right away.'

'When was she on?'

'She was on the news. I just finished watching. I went next door where they have a set.'

'Are you expecting her back?'

Peg raised her long holder, took a draw on her cigarette. 'I'm not sure,' she said. 'And I'll tell you the truth, Michael, I've been having some second thoughts.'

'What do you mean?'

'Well, she's going to be the woman of the hour, and all that. The media will all be after her. But do I want her working here? I mean, it's all very well to play Joan of Arc, but I don't want to be sitting here waiting for some gunman to walk in the door of this place and blow us all to smithereens. You see my point?'

'I do,' he said. 'Have you told her that?'
'Not yet. But I think I will.'

In the lobby of the Clarence, Rory Burke met him as he came through the door. 'Where have you been? There's two reporters waiting for you and the phone's been ringing for the last hour, ITV from London, and the BBC, and even Americans, CBS Television, they're all after you. What's going on?'

But even as Rory was telling him this two men came out of the bar and came up to him. 'Are you Mr Dillon?'

'Yes.'

'I'm from the *Independent*. I wonder, could we talk to you?'

He saw now that the other man had a camera. 'Just a minute,' he said to them and, turning to Rory, led him aside. 'Rory, I was talking to London earlier. They want you to take over as manager here. It's temporary, mind you. Anyway, we'll talk about it later. But I won't be working here any more. All right? You're manager *pro tem*. OK?'

Rory's eyes widened in joy then narrowed in caution. 'You're not leaving us?'

'I'll tell you about it later,' he said again and turned to the waiting reporters. 'All right, gentlemen. If you'll come up to my office?'

The reporter had an English accent, so Dillon deduced he was from the London *Independent*, and not the Irish newspaper of the same name. The photographer was local. He spoke up as they went towards the mezzanine stairs. 'I wonder, could I just take a picture of you now, sir? Maybe outside the hotel?'

'I don't know if I want my picture taken. What's this about?'

The photographer looked at the English reporter who gave him a warning stare. 'Sorry, now,' the photographer said. 'Whenever it suits you, sir. No hurry.' They went upstairs in silence and when Dillon showed them into his office the photographer walked to the window, and stood, looking out, as though divorcing himself from any further involvement.

'Your wife was on television a little while ago,' the reporter said. 'I suppose you know about that?'

'I heard she was on television. I don't know what she said.'

'Well, it's an extraordinary story, isn't it? I mean, it must have been a terrible dilemma for you, mustn't it?'

'What dilemma?'

'I mean, as she said, your having to choose between her life and a lot of other people's lives. She – she just mentioned it, of course, on television. Didn't really go into it. It was a news broadcast, there wasn't time. I wonder if you could tell us more about it now?'

'I don't think I want to discuss it,' Dillon said. 'I don't want to say anything until I've spoken to her.'

'I see. Yes, of course. And when will you be speaking to her, Mr Dillon? Could we, perhaps, talk after that?'

'I don't know. I don't know where she is at the moment.'

The photographer turned back from the window. 'They were taking her over to the BBC on Ormeau Avenue,' he said. 'That was just a wee while ago.'

'Thanks,' Dillon said. 'Well, if you'll excuse me.'

'Are you going over there?' the reporter asked. 'Could we, perhaps, give you a lift?'

'Thank you. I have a car.' He went to the door and waited while, reluctantly, they took their leave.

As they went out Maggie Donlon came in. 'What's this I hear about your leaving us? Is it true?'

'Did you get your car back all right?' he asked.

'Yes, thanks, Michael. Listen, I heard about your wife being on TV. What a story! Are you leaving here because they're after you, is that it?'

'Who said I was leaving?'

'Our new manager.' She laughed. '*Mister* Burke.'

'He doesn't waste any time,' Dillon said. 'Listen, Maggie, I have to run. What was it you wanted?'

'I just wanted to ask you, because if he's going to be the manager I'm leaving now.'

'It's only temporary,' he said, 'don't worry,' and, waving to her, he went past her and ran down to the lobby.

'Mr Dillon, you're wanted on the phone,' one of the desk clerks called out, but he shook his head and ran outside to his rented car. The BBC on Ormeau Avenue was only minutes away. There, uniformed commissionaires put him through a security check before admitting him to the entrance lobby.

Once inside, he realised he did not know who to ask for. When he had been here before it had always been to see Andrea. Would Andrea know where to find Moira? He had no other choice. At reception he asked for Miss Baxter. They telephoned, then told him, 'She's in a meeting, sir. Who will I say is calling?'

'My name is Dillon,' he said. 'Actually, I'm looking for my wife. She's supposed to be here for some show or other.'

The middle-aged woman on the reception desk looked up at him with new interest. 'Is that the lady – ? Oh, yes, of course. I think they took her to Studio Six.'

The other woman on reception said, 'I think she's in make-up now.'

'It's urgent,' he said. 'I have to see her right away.'

The women looked at each other, then one of them said, 'Do you have any identification, sir?' He showed his driver's licence.

Both of them looked at it, then the older woman signalled to a commissionaire. 'Harry, will you take this gentleman to make-up? It's for a guest called Mrs Dillon.'

'Thank you,' he said. He followed the commissionaire to the lift and went up. The commissionaire, an elderly man, said that it was a nice day but the forecast was for more rain. Then, with the lift still moving upwards, he said, 'You're that lady's husband, then?'

Dillon nodded.

'I heard her on the news on telly,' the commissionaire said. 'She's dead right, you know. Somebody has to speak up. I mean against both sides – the UDA as well. Them and the IRA, there's no difference if you ask me.' The lift had stopped. 'This way, sir.'

He followed the commissionaire along a corridor past a seedy looking room containing a coffee machine, sofas and a table with magazines. At the end of the corridor he saw the make-up room, a sort of barbershop, with swivel chairs facing lighted mirrors. In the make-up room two young men and a girl who carried a clipboard were clustered around a woman in a white coat. When Dillon entered the room they separated, looking back at him. At that moment, he saw that the woman in the white coat was putting make-up on someone seated in one of the swivel chairs. The someone was Moira.

'There you are, sir,' the commissionaire said. 'I'll be waitin' for you when you're ready.'

He went in. Moira saw him in the mirror, but did not turn around. She leaned back in the chair as the woman dabbed suntan make-up on her brow. The people who were with Moira eyed him cautiously.

'Can I speak to you for a moment?' Dillon said to her.

One of the young men at once came forward, looking at him suspiciously. 'Excuse me, sir. What is this about?'

'I'm her husband.'

At once the girl with the clipboard came up, smiling and excited. 'Mr Dillon? We've been trying to track you down. How do you do, my name's Meg Harris, I'm the producer, we're just about to do an interview with your wife. We're also taping this segment for CBS, in America; anyway, I'm sure you're not interested in all that. What I'm asking you is, will you join Mrs Dillon in the interview? That would be super.'

He looked at Moira who had her eyes closed as the make-up woman dabbed powder on her eyelids. 'If I could just talk to her for a minute, in private?' he said to the girl producer.

The make-up woman at once said to Moira, 'I'm nearly done, love. Just one more wee touch. There you are, love.'

Moira sat up and the make-up woman helped her remove the smock which protected her dress. The girl whispered something to the two young men, then said, 'Well, we have a few minutes, if you want to talk. If you'll come this way, there's a visitor's waiting room.'

He looked at Moira who did not look at him, but turned back to the mirror, inspected herself, then said to the make-up woman, 'Could I have a brush?'

'Certainly, love.'

Intent, as though she were alone in her own bedroom, Moira took the brush to her long hair, tugging it, fluffing it out behind.

'That's lovely, now,' the make-up woman said as Moira handed back the brush. Moira thanked her and then they went down the corridor to the seedy room which Dillon had passed earlier.

'We'll wait outside,' the girl producer said, shutting them in. Through the glass panel of the door Dillon could see them waiting in the corridor, the two young men laughing at something the girl producer said, the elderly commissionaire standing a little off from the others.

Moira walked over to one of the shabby sofas and sat down. 'Did you see me on the news?' she asked. Her voice was neutral.

'No, but I heard about it. I notice you didn't bother to ask me before you got us into this.'

'Got you into what?' She had taken her mirror out of her bag and was looking at her lips.

'What Peg Wilton calls your Joan of Arc bit. Are you trying to become a martyr, is that it?'

'I thought you were the one who wanted to make a martyr of me?' she said.

'What do you mean?'

'When you rang up the police about the bomb.'

'All right, all right,' he said. 'Look, that's done, it's over. But think about what you're doing now. Are you trying to get yourself killed?'

'I'm doing what I think is right. Just as you did when you phoned the police. Are you going to come on this interview with me, or not?'

'No,' he said. 'Listen, my transfer's come through. I'm going to London tomorrow.'

'Are you, now?' she said sarcastically. 'Well, if you do, I suppose that's the end of us.'

'Look,' he said. 'I want to talk to you about that.'

'About what?' she said, and suddenly he saw fear in her face.

'About us.'

She looked down at her bag. She put the mirror back in it and shut the bag with a click. 'What was her name again? The one you were holding hands with this morning?'

'Her name is Andrea Baxter.'

'Is she going to miss you?'

He did not answer. Suddenly, she began to sob. 'Oh, Christ,' she said. 'Go away, will you?'

Ashamed, he turned and looked at the glass-panelled door. The young men and the girl producer were talking to each other but it was pretend-talk. They were watching Moira as, sobbing, she took a Kleenex from her purse. The girl producer caught his eye and mimed, pointing to her wristwatch. He went to the door and opened it.

'Is everything all right?' the girl asked.

From behind him Moira answered, 'Fine. Are we ready, then?'

The girl looked at him. 'Are you joining us, Mr Dillon? If you are we'll have to send you to make-up for a moment.'

'No.' He signalled to the elderly commissionaire who waited further down the corridor. 'Will we go, then?'

'Right, sir,' the commissionaire said.

'Sure you won't change your mind?' one of the young men

asked. 'The interview would be much stronger with both of you.'

He shook his head, then looked back. Moira, standing behind him, said to the girl, 'Am I all right? My face, I mean?'

'Yes, you're grand,' the girl said.

The young men had moved ahead of him and he realised that they were all going to the same bank of lifts. As they waited for the lift to come, he turned to Moira. 'Where will you be tonight? At the house?'

She hesitated, then said, 'I might stay with Peg, if she'll let me.'

He thought of Peg's remark, an hour ago. Peg would not be keen to have a guest who might have a visit from the IRA. 'And, if not,' he said, 'where else could I reach you?'

'At Mama's. Are you going to the house?'

'No,' he said. 'I've taken my clothes.'

He was aware that the two young men, the girl producer and the commissionaire were listening to every word. We have become somebody they will talk about. We are in the news.

The lift arrived. When the lift door opened, Moira walked in, and stood, with her back to him. The young men followed. The girl producer bobbed her head at him apologetically. 'We're going up,' she said.

The lift door shut. The elderly commissionaire looked up at the clock-like indicator. 'There's just the one lift workin',' he said. 'It'll be back down in a minute.'

They stood in silence, watching the indicator ascend. 'So it was Pottinger they were after?' the commissionaire asked.

'It seems so.'

The indicator stopped, then began to descend. 'That's the thing of it, isn't it?' the commissionaire said. 'It's not the ones that ought to get hurt who gets hurt.'

*

129

At the security gate of the hotel, Jack McGowan, one of the security men, came out to open up for him. 'Your father's waitin' for you, sir. I let him park in the front. Is that OK?'

It was not 'OK' but his father, like a dog marking its territory by urinating, insisted on claiming some special privilege each time he set foot in the hotel. His father craved recognition. He would prefer to eat in a bad restaurant which gave him the best table than in a good one where he was not known. Now, when Dillon entered the lobby, the doorman came up to tell him that his father was waiting for him in the bar. He went into the bar which was crowded with lunch-time drinkers and saw his father at the far end of the bar counter, trapping Mickey, the head barman, as audience for one of his tales.

'Ah, there he is,' his father said, waving to him. Mickey, relieved to be released from listening, also waved and said, 'Will you have something, Mr Dillon?'

'Could you order me a sandwich and a beer?' he asked Mickey, then turned to his father. 'Have you had lunch, Daddy?'

'Not hungry,' his father said and beckoned to a table at the far end of the bar as though he, not Dillon, were in charge here. They sat. His father wore his usual country squire costume of ancient tweed suit, checked shirt, wool tie and polished brogues. In his hand he held a small whisky which he had not touched.

'Didn't you get my messages?' he asked. 'You might have called back.'

'I'm sorry, Daddy. It's been bedlam here the last twenty-four hours.'

'I can imagine,' his father said. 'Anyway, when we didn't hear from you I decided to come to town today and do a few errands. And there I was, sitting in the car, driving in from Derry, when I heard Moira being interviewed on the car radio. My God, what a story!'

His father had always loved a drama. This was a tale he would tell in years to come. But he sensed something else, some disquiet in his father's manner. 'What an awful business it is,' his father said. 'But, Michael, do you think it's wise to be telling it to the whole world the way she is?'

'I didn't hear her. I've no idea what she said.'

'She didn't consult you?'

'No.'

'Why not? Is it because of what you did?'

His father's rosy-cheeked, bonhomous face gave no hint of what his father knew. Does he know about us, how can he? 'Because of what I *did*?'

'Well, I mean ringing the police. Saving Pottinger's hide. They could have killed her. I think if I were Moira I'd have mixed feelings about that.'

'What are you talking about? I wasn't just saving Pottinger's life. The bomb was under the dining-room of the hotel. God knows how many people would have been killed.'

'Still,' his father said. 'Not to belabour the point, but she might be angry with you.'

'No, she wasn't angry. She said she thought I did the right thing.' But, as he told his father this, it came to him that Moira had done the interview after she saw him holding hands with Andrea. 'What *did* she say? I mean when you heard her on the radio?'

'Well, she told the whole story, more or less, about the two of you and how they treated you that night. And she said that the IRA are thugs and so on, and how everybody's afraid to speak out. She ended up saying that if Catholics are calling for "Brits out" they should also call for "IRA out", because we'll have no peace until we get rid of them.'

'Well, she's right about that,' Dillon said.

'That's got nothing to do with it,' his father said. 'It's your life she's risking.'

'What about her own life? She's as much at risk as I am.'

'Nonsense,' his father said. 'It's you they'll come after. You double-crossed them. They might want to get back at you.'

One of the waitresses had come into the bar and now approached them, carrying a tray on which there was a beer and a sandwich. 'It's for you, sir, isn't it?' she said, placing it in front of him. As she did, he saw his father at last take a sip of his whisky.

'They're transferring me to England,' he said. 'As a safety measure.'

His father seemed stunned by this news. 'The Yanks . . . Well, yes, that's . . . I suppose it's wise. Where are they sending you?'

'The Ormonde in London as one of the assistant managers.'

'But you were manager here. That's quite a step down. What a bloody mess. Bloody Pottinger.'

'It's all right, Daddy,' he said. 'I want to go back. It could be a step up eventually.'

'How does Moira feel about going?'

'I don't know yet,' he lied. He began to eat his sandwich. His father, agitated, lit a cigarette and watched him eat. Bloody Pottinger, his father had said. As usual, he had found someone to blame. His father, although a Northerner, had chosen to live in the Republic of Ireland because, there, he was no longer a member of a Catholic minority which his Ulster Protestant acquaintances looked down on and despised. His father, like most Ulster Catholics of his generation, held no brief for the present IRA but reserved his true enmity and ingrained bigotry for Pottinger and the extremists of the Ulster Defence Association. The IRA might be planning to murder his son but still, in the last analysis, his father, irrationally, felt that Pottinger was to blame.

'So when are they sending you to London?' his father asked.

'Any time now. Tomorrow, maybe.'

As he said this, he saw Rory Burke come to the bar entrance, look round, and hurry towards him. 'Michael,' Rory said. 'Glad I found you. Listen, the contractor's here and I don't know what plans you made about the repairs.' He turned to Dillon's father. 'Hello, Mr Dillon. Sorry to interrupt.'

'That's all right,' his father said. 'Don't worry about me. I know what these things are like.'

'Can you come now?' Rory asked.

'Go ahead, Michael,' his father said. 'And give us a ring before you go off to London. Your mother will want to talk to you. Don't forget, now.'

Normally, when he and his father met or parted they did not embrace or exchange handshakes. But now as he rose to leave, his father stood up and gripped him by the shoulders, pressing him close. 'Take care of yourself,' his father said, his voice shaken with emotion. 'And where can I reach Moira? I want to talk to her.'

'Try our house. Goodbye, Daddy. Thanks for coming.'

'Keep in touch,' his father said. 'God bless.' There were tears in his eyes.

As they left the bar Rory said, 'Are you worried? I suppose you must be. By the way, they say your wife was terrific on TV this morning. Everybody's talking about it.'

'Is he here himself, the contractor?' he asked, changing the subject.

'McAnally? Yes. He's out at the back. I don't even know if it's a fixed bid or what, on the repairs. Is it?'

'No, it isn't. I should have filled you in on it. Listen, Rory, I realise now I can't hand over without spending at least a day with you.'

'Good. I'm relieved,' Rory said.

They went out to the car-park. The English reporter who had tried to interview him earlier came up. 'Mr Dillon? Perhaps you can give me a few minutes now?'

'I'm sorry. I'm very busy.'

'Have you spoken to your wife yet? You remember you promised me an interview after you'd spoken to her?'

'I don't remember promising you an interview.'

The reporter looked at him. 'As a matter of fact, I came right over to see you, because I've just been talking to your wife. She told me you actually *saw* one of the IRA men. I mean, saw his face. Is that correct?'

Dillon looked over at Rory. *Oh, my God*, he thought. *Everybody will know it now.*

'Did she say that on television?' he asked.

'Not as far as I know. She just told it to me. So, I wanted to verify it with you before we print anything.'

'I don't know what she's talking about,' Dillon said.

'What are you trying to do?' Rory broke in indignantly. 'Are you trying to get this man killed?'

'I just asked him a question,' the reporter said.

'Look, I can't talk to you now, I told you, I'm very busy.' Dillon walked on towards McAnally, the contractor, who was standing near the bomb damage, giving orders to two of his men. The English reporter turned and went back to his car.

Rory, hurrying along beside Dillon, looked at him sideways. 'None of my business,' he said, 'but she's taking a lot on herself, isn't she? Your wife, I mean. What do the police say?'

'Look, Rory, I don't know. Let's drop it, OK?'

'Sorry, now,' Rory said. They had reached McAnally. The talk turned to the work to be done but Dillon found himself unable to pay attention. When they had finished with McAnally they went upstairs to Dillon's office where he was to show Rory the personnel files. In his office, the phone was ringing. He picked it up.

'It's for you on line two,' the operator said.

'Who is it?'

'They wouldn't say. They said it was private.'

'Right,' he said. 'I'll take it.'

'Mr Dillon?' a girl's voice said. She spoke with a Belfast accent.

'Yes.'

'Hold on, please.'

'Michael Dillon?' It was a male voice.

'Speaking.'

'You've been speakin' a bit too much,' the voice said. 'Is it publicity, you want, the pair of you? Because, if it is, we can give you more publicity. You mightn't be around to read about it, though.'

There was a pause.

'Did you hear me, Dillon?'

'Yes.'

'Right, then.'

The line went dead. He replaced the receiver. Rory looked up from the desk. 'Everything all right?'

He nodded. 'Are you all right?' Rory said again.

It was then that he realised he was shaking. 'Yes,' he said. 'Yes. But, listen, Rory. I have to get in touch with Moira. Maybe we can do this a bit later on in the day?'

'Sure. I'll be here,' Rory said, rising to leave.

He found his address book and dialled a number. 'Peg, it's Michael Dillon. Has Moira come back yet?'

'As a matter of fact she just walked in the door,' Peg's voice said. 'Do you want to speak to her? Here, I'll pass her over.'

'Who is it?' he heard Moira ask before she picked up the receiver. Then she said, 'Michael, I'm busy now. I told you I'd come up to the hotel later. All right?'

'No. I have to see you now. It's important. I'll come over.'

'Wait a minute,' Moira said. She put down the phone, then came back. 'We'll be next door, Peg and I. We're going to have a cup of tea. It's a place called the Bon-Bon.'

'I want to speak to you alone.'

'I haven't had any lunch,' she said crossly. 'Do you want to see me, or don't you?'

'I'll be there.'

To enter the city's central shopping area he was forced to leave his car in a car-park three streets away. As he passed through the security check at the entrance to the pedestrian malls a teenage boy wearing a T-shirt with 'U2' blazoned on it waited at the other side of the security gate. The boy looked at him, and as he went down the crowded shopping street he saw the boy follow him. The Bon-Bon was a tea-shop, next door to the large toyshop which he had passed that morning. As before, a number of children were peering in at the display of moving toy cars. Dillon stopped by this window and, looking back, saw the boy idling by a sports shop further up the street. He kept looking at the boy. The boy turned slightly and looked in his direction, then, realising Dillon was watching him, he went in at the entrance to the sports shop as if to make a purchase. At once, Dillon ducked into the Bon-Bon tea-shop.

It was a large place, crowded with women having afternoon tea, and a long line of customers at the counters, buying cakes and pastries. There were a number of children in the shop, so it was noisy. Ignoring the hostess's offer to seat him, Dillon searched around and saw Moira at a table by the window. She was alone. She did not look up when he came to her. A half-empty teacup sat at the place opposite hers. 'Is Peg here?' he asked, indicating the cup.

'She just left,' Moira said. In the centre of the table was a plate of cream pastries and at Moira's place was a half-eaten slice of chocolate cake. 'Sit down,' she said. 'What is it you want?'

He sat, facing her. 'I just had a phone call from our friends of the other night. Warning me that we're talking too much.'

'So?' she said. 'They don't like it. Good.'

'Look, Moira, what are you trying to do? Get us both killed? Didn't that police Inspector warn us not to tell anybody that I'd seen Kev's face?'

'I'm not taking orders from the police,' she said, and, with her fork, cut herself another mouthful of the rich cake.

'That's not the point. If the police are trying to catch them, you're just tipping them off. They'll hide him now. They'll send him down South or out of the country.'

She paused, the forkful of cake in the air, then put it down, untasted. 'You're right,' she said. 'Damn it, I didn't think of that.'

'Did you mention it on telly? I mean about Kev?'

'No, I just told that one reporter. An English one. OK, I won't tell anybody else.'

'It's too late,' he said. 'What do you think they called me for?'

'Did they mention that particular thing?' she asked.

'No.'

'So it wasn't that,' she said. 'I'll tell you why they rang you up. Because I was on telly. Because this story about what they did to us is going to be all over Europe and America.'

'Great. More publicity for them. Just what they want.'

'Wrong,' she said. 'I'm speaking up *against* them.'

'Who are you kidding? You're doing it because you love all this – people seeing you on the box and your picture in the newspapers.'

'You *are* stupid,' she said. 'And I used to think you were bright. I'm doing it because, for the first time in my life, I have a chance to change things. Maybe that's why people go into politics.'

'Or why they go into the IRA.'

'Look, Michael, let me ask you something. What do you think my life's been until now? It's cooking meals for you, doing teaching jobs I didn't want to do and worrying about my looks and why I'm losing them. That's been my life, hasn't it? And now, finding out that you don't give a damn about me, that you're like every other man I've ever known, you don't care whether I have a brain or not, you don't know me, you don't want to know what makes me tick – all you ever wanted to know was what am I like in bed, what do other people think of me, do they envy you because you sleep with me? Isn't that it?'

'Yes,' he said. 'Yes, I suppose it is. But, Moira, anything you say on the telly or in the newspapers isn't going to change things here. The only thing it's going to change is your own life. All this blathering on telly has already cost you your job with Peg.'

'Who told you that?'

'Peg did. This morning. And I don't blame her. Why should she have to be worrying that a couple of IRA men are going to walk into her shop and kill her?'

As he spoke, he remembered the boy outside. He looked out the window. The boy was still there. He was now standing behind the peering children at the toyshop next door, pretending to watch the display of moving mechanical cars.

'Look over there,' he said to her. 'See the one in the U2 T-shirt. He's following me. This is the IRA we're mixed up with. You know very well we could be killed. Is that what you want?'

'That's a good question,' she said, 'coming from you. What do *you* want? Did you want to see me killed the other day? Supposing it had been your girlfriend the IRA were holding in the house? Would you have picked up the phone and called the police? Would you?'

Suddenly, the tea-shop noises seemed unbearably loud. Women's voices, the clatter of dishes, children crying. 'Yes,' he said.

'You're a liar. You wanted me dead.'

'I did not.'

'Tell me. Is she going with you to England?'

'Yes.'

'So, it's serious,' she said. She turned away from him and looked out the window, her face, in profile, still as the image on a coin. 'You want a divorce, then?'

'Yes.'

She sat, still looking out the window. 'I hope they shoot you,' she said. She bent down and picked up her handbag which sat on the floor. She stood up, caught her breath in a sudden gasp, and then, at last, looked at him. 'No,' she said. 'I hope they shoot me.'

She walked away, going to the cashier, pulling a five pound note from her purse. She handed it to the cashier, did not wait for change and went out into the street. He got up to go after her, but, when he came out into the street and looked left and right, she was gone. As he stood, searching for her in the moving mass of people, he saw the boy still standing outside the toyshop. A young girl came running up the street, running towards the boy. The boy smiled and they kissed. He put his arm around her and they walked off, innocent lovers, disappearing into the crowd.

EIGHT

At first, seeing the two men standing by the reception desk, Dillon took them for guests. They were speaking to the desk clerk, but then one of them, seeing Dillon, came up to him, smiling. This man was middle aged and well turned out in grey flannels, a navy blazer with a white handkerchief tucked in the breast pocket, a gleaming white shirt and a club tie. 'Mr Dillon,' he said, as though he expected to be recognised. When he saw that Dillon did not know him, he added quickly, 'Detective Inspector Randall. We met yesterday at your house.'

'Oh, of course,' Dillon said. The second man, who stood behind Randall, was tall and bald. He wore a grey tweed suit and thin round-lensed steel glasses which emphasised the nakedness of his skull. 'This is Chief Detective Inspector Norton of the Special Branch,' Randall said.

'Sorry to disturb you,' the Chief Inspector said. 'I'm sure you're very busy.'

'No, no.' Dillon remembered that Rory was using his office. He gestured towards the bar. 'What about a drink?'

'The bar looks a bit crowded,' the Chief Inspector said.

'There's a lounge on the mezzanine,' he told them. 'We can talk there.'

In the mezzanine lounge, the policemen moved as by instinct towards a corner banquette where they settled in with their backs to the wall. They refused a drink and ordered coffee. The only other customers in the lounge were a noisy family group and a middle-aged man who sat up at the bar watching the television screen overhead.

The Chief Inspector glanced over at the television set. 'I hear your wife will be on the six o'clock news.' He looked at his watch. 'Maybe we'll see her.'

'She was on earlier today,' Randall said. 'I missed it. And she's in all the papers. Did nobody ask to interview you?'

'I didn't want to be interviewed.' He saw them exchange glances. 'I'm sorry about her mentioning that I'd seen that boy's face,' he said.

'Who did she mention it to?' the Chief Inspector asked.

'A reporter from the *Independent*. The English paper.'

'When was that?'

'This morning.'

'I haven't seen anything about it in the papers,' Inspector Randall said.

'The *Independent*,' the Chief Inspector said, as if noting it down. 'Was that the only time she said it?'

'I'm not sure.'

'The fact is,' the Chief Inspector said, 'we have a good notion of who the one called Kev might be.'

'Oh.'

'You're going to be here? In Belfast?' the Chief Inspector asked.

'No, I've asked for a transfer to one of our hotels in London. I'm to leave tomorrow, or the day after.'

The Chief Inspector leaned his bald head against the leather back of the banquette and stared up at the ceiling. His long, flat-tipped fingers stroked his bald skull as though he were concentrating, trying to solve some mathematical problem. 'Well, that's all right,' he said at last. 'We could always bring

141

you back over again. Yes. Your wife's going with you, I presume?'

'No, that's not settled yet.'

'Is that so?' the Chief Inspector said.

'Well, it's a personal matter. Besides, she's never wanted to live in England.'

The Chief Inspector smiled. Again he leaned back, stroking his bald skull. 'I know how she feels,' he said. 'The quality of life over there is not as good as it is here. The ordinary schools are far below ours in standards. And they have more drugs and mixed populations. And it's crowded over there, isn't it? I can understand her.' He sat up now, looking at Dillon. 'You know, you never can tell about these things,' he said. 'But, based on the bad publicity the IRA's been getting lately, killing innocent bystanders, women and children and so on, I think you'd be the one who's at risk, not your wife. It wouldn't look well for them to be shooting her, a young woman like that, who people have just seen on television. I'd say you're the one they'd want. You're the one who phoned us. And you're the one who saw that boy's face.'

'They rang me up today to warn me,' he said.

'Did they?' Inspector Randall said.

'When was that?' the Chief Inspector asked.

'This afternoon.'

'And what did they say?'

He told them. They looked at each other and then the Chief Inspector said, 'Of course, that might not have been the IRA.'

'What do you mean?'

'Well, in the past, we've found that quite a few of those calls come from some fellows in a pub, maybe IRA supporters just deciding to ring up on their own. They do it for badness.'

'I see.'

'Anyway,' the Chief Inspector said, 'what we came around to ask you is this. If we do bring a suspect in, would you be willing to identify him and testify at his trial?'

They both looked at him. 'Well, I only saw his face for a moment,' he said.

They were still looking at him, waiting. 'Well,' he said. 'Yes, I suppose I could.'

'Good. Thank you.' The Chief Inspector stood up. Inspector Randall also stood, smiling now. 'Thank you, Mr Dillon,' Randall said. 'We're grateful for your help. By the way, do you have a London address?'

'You can reach me at the Ormonde Hotel.'

'Very nice, too,' the Chief Inspector said, and laughed.

'Oh, I'm not living there, I'm working there. I don't have a home address yet.'

'Well, thank you again,' the Chief Inspector said. He looked at his watch, then at the television set. 'I'm afraid we can't wait for the TV news, but, as I said, we hear your wife's going to be on. Thanks for the coffee.'

He watched them as they walked towards the staircase. Randall could be a bank manager, the Chief Inspector a country schoolteacher. The men they hunted also wore the masks of normal life. That middle-aged man sitting at the bar, who eyed them as they went past, could be someone who had spent years in Long Kesh prison, who had ordered other men to be shot or crippled, who had planned the botched assassination of Pottinger, who, seeing him with these policemen, might now decide that he should be put to death. It was a world of men in masks whose true identity could not be guessed. And now, to one of them, he had been asked to put a face.

The bar waitress came to take away the coffee cups and Dillon heard the familiar voice of the television newsreader announcing the six o'clock news. He got up, went to the bar, and sat two stools away from the middle-aged man who was still its only occupant. As he did, Tommy Spence, the barman on duty, came out from his pantry. 'Can I get you something, Mr Dillon?'

'Thanks, Tommy. I'll have a gin and tonic.'

There had been another earthquake in Mexico, a Japanese

143

Prime Minister had resigned because of a scandal, a government inquiry had been set up to investigate the latest incident of football hooliganism. Two men, a young businessman and an older one, joined them at the bar. A group of six people came into the lounge and were seated. The men in this group wore rented morning clothes and were a little drunk. The women carrying crushed bouquets of flowers were bridesmaids and attendants in what had been a wedding party. Laughing and ordering drinks, the group paid no attention to the television news.

And then, the familiar voice said, 'In Northern Ireland today . . . ' At once the room became quiet. It was as though that other world of television did not exist. Now they watched in silence, as the screen showed the actual hotel they were sitting in, then the bomb-damaged car-park. The newsreader said that the bombing had now been established as an attempt to assassinate the Reverend Alun Pottinger and that the wife of the hotel manager had been held hostage in her home while her husband had been forced to drive to the hotel with a bomb in his car. 'The wife, Mrs Michael Dillon,' the newsreader's voice said, and suddenly on the television screen, seated in a studio, was Moira, looking beautiful and distraught and, at the same time, angry. A woman television reporter asked her if she had been frightened and Moira, in close-up, looked at the camera and said, 'I was but I'm not any more. I want to see them caught and punished. I think it's time for ordinary people to stand up to the IRA and get rid of them.' Abruptly, the screen flashed to a picture of the Houses of Parliament and the newsreader said, 'In the debate today in the House over short-range nuclear missiles . . . ' At once it was as though the rest of the news had been turned off. The room swelled with excited talk. A voice from the wedding party said, 'Imagine sittin' here in the hotel and it on television.' Another voice said, 'She's good-lookin', the wife.' Dillon saw Tommy, the barman, look at him as he overheard this remark. Tommy shook his head and smiled. The middle-aged man next to Dillon leaned over. 'Excuse me, did I hear that you're Mr Dillon?' Dillon nodded. He looked at his barely touched drink and decided to leave it. 'It must have been a terrible experience,' the man said. The two businessmen further down the bar had been listening to this and now studied Dillon as though he were a celebrity. Dillon signalled and said, 'Thanks, Tommy. Put that on my chit.' He got up and walked across the lounge. By the way they looked at him, he knew the wedding party had also learned of his identity. The room was now quiet, the only sound the unlistened-to voice of the television newsreader continuing with the unwatched world news.

Leaving the lounge, he went down the corridor to his office. She had only been on screen for a moment. She had not mentioned that he had seen Kev's face. It was not a big story. Nobody had been killed. By tomorrow it would be forgotten. Then he remembered the English reporter. He is the only one she told. It will be his exclusive story, so of course he'll write it up. I must get the evening papers.

But when he went into his office he saw a British tabloid and two local newspapers lying on the sofa. Rory, who was on the phone, waved to him as he sat down. The tabloid on top of the pile had a large headline and Moira's photograph, 'IRA OUT, SAYS HOSTAGE HOUSEWIFE'.

The story was short. There was no mention of what he feared. He picked up the first local newspaper, reading at speed, looking for the telling sentence. Rory, who had finished on the phone, called over. 'You're in the news, all right, aren't you?'

He nodded. He finished the story. There was no mention of his having seen Kev's face. He picked up the other local paper, did not find it there either. Perhaps the police had managed to keep that statement out?

'Are you OK?' Rory asked. 'You look as if you could do with a drink.'

'No, I'm all right. I'm just going down to get the English papers.'

But by the time he reached the news-stand in the lobby he realised that if the English papers carried the story it would be in tomorrow's editions. He would have to wait till then.

As he turned back from the news-stand, Andrea came into the lobby and saw him. 'Are you all right, Michael? What's the matter? You look terrible.' She kissed him. 'Listen, I'm going to take you home,' she said. 'I'll cook supper. Can you come now?'

He nodded. He went to the house phone and called Rory. 'Rory, I'll see you in the morning. I may not be able to leave for London for a day or two.'

'Oh? Why's that?' He sensed Rory's unease at this news.

'Nothing important,' he said. 'I'll talk to you later.'

He went back into the lobby and was again aware that people were looking at him. He said to Andrea, 'Let's get out of here.' Jack, the doorman on duty, pushed open the revolving doors for them. He thought he saw a knowing smile on Jack's face. Was it already a subject of gossip among the staff that he had spent last night in the Jacuzzi suite with a girl? Until now, he and Andrea had been careful not to be seen when they spent an hour or two together in one of the rooms here. Until now, his private life had been unknown to others.

When he came out of the hotel with Andrea, Peggy Harris, one of the receptionists, was coming up the driveway. She nodded to him. 'Good-night, Michael.' She then looked at Andrea with great curiosity.

Maybe Peggy knows. But what does it matter? It did matter. He had not thought of it before. Once people knew he was having an affair, they would suspect his motive in risking Moira's life.

''Night, Mr Dillon,' said Billy Craig, opening the security gate. ''Night, Miss.'

Does Billy know? If the others do, he does. Everyone knows.

*

Andrea had arranged that they would spend the evening alone in the flat. She had never cooked for him before and now he watched, surprised, as she made a *béarnaise* sauce for their steaks, moving in the cramped kitchen with the assurance of someone who knows exactly what she must do. She had bought wine, prepared a salad, and set the table, and when he complimented her she turned to him, smiling, and said, 'Aren't you relieved that I can cook? We'll be doing this all the time from now on.'

'I hope so.'

'What's the matter? What's wrong?'

'Well, I was thinking,' he said. 'Moira saying that I could identify one of the IRA men. That could put you in danger, I mean, being with me.'

She turned back to the grill, busy, as though she had not heard him. 'Come on,' she said. 'Open the wine.'

When they went into the dining-room which was a makeshift alcove off the hall, she lit two candles on the table and said to him, 'Now, stop it, will you? You said yourself it wasn't on television and it's not in any of the papers. I'll bet the police have managed to keep it out.'

'We won't know until the morning. I suppose that's what's getting to me.'

'Remember, this is part of Great Britain,' she said. 'And the powers that be in Britain are pretty good at keeping the Press in line. Look on the bright side. Moira knows about us now. You've told her. It's over. You're leaving, you're getting away from here, and we're going to be together. We should be celebrating.'

'We are,' he said. He got up, came around the table and kissed her. 'Sorry.'

'You can stay here tonight,' she said. 'It's a single bed, though. I'm warning you.'

*

Shortly after one a.m. a summer thunderstorm filled the night sky. Sheet lightning flashed like strobe lights in the long, low-ceilinged attic where they slept. Dillon lay with Andrea in his arms, seeing her face ghost-white in the lightning's blaze, her eyes closed, her breathing steady as a patient under ether. In the room below he could hear her flatmates moving about, closing the windows against the coming rain. In the pallor of the storm he stared at the walls; they were like the walls in a nursery, taped with drawings, posters, photographs. Old over-coats and an umbrella hung from pegs behind the door. Metal shelves held rows of cassettes, a teddy bear, a tape recorder and a player. Books and magazines were scattered on a long table under the large skylight window. In this room, with Andrea in his arms, it seemed to him that he was already in another country. But thunder, contradicting him, shook the room with a noise like a bomb exploding. He thought of Moira, lying in what bed tonight? At home, or at her mother's, or where? Was she awake now and thinking vengeful thoughts? Again, the pallid lightning filled the room, blazing on a poster tacked to the attic beam above him. It was a poster for U2, the Irish rock group. Wild youths in silhouette, a ghost image, gone. Again, in the dark, he listened for the second barrel of thunder. He thought of the boy he had seen earlier that day, wearing a U2 T-shirt, the one who had waited for his girl outside the toyshop, the one he had feared was a scout for the IRA. That was the real damage in all this. Never to know. Try not to worry, Andrea said. But how can I not worry? Not to know. That is the real fear.

The thunder came. Rain fell, heavy as pellets on the attic roof. At last, Andrea stirred in her sleep. He held her, wondering would she wake, wanting her to wake, wanting her with him. But she slept on, far away, in a peaceful world that had shut him out.

Next morning, unexpectedly, the see-saw of his emotions lifted him high. When he drove Andrea to work, he stopped and bought the English papers. *The Times*, the *Guardian* and the *Daily Telegraph* carried stories saying the police believed the hotel bombing had been an attempt to assassinate Pottinger, but gave no details of his or Moira's role in the affair. The *Independent*, whose reporters had tried to interview him yesterday, carried a longer story which described how he and Moira had been held hostage overnight and said that he had notified the police at once when forced to drive to the hotel with a bomb in his car. The tabloids turned it into a small human interest story, 'HUSBAND'S AGONIZING CHOICE', with a picture of Moira looking beautiful, and smiling at the camera.

But none of the papers made any mention of Moira's saying he could identify one of the terrorists. 'I was right,' Andrea said, as they sat in the car, riffling through the pages. 'Official secrets, D notices, whatever it is they can do here to muzzle the Press, they did it again.'

'Wait a minute,' he said. 'Whose side are you on?'

She laughed and threw aside the newspaper. 'So, stop worrying,' she said. 'It's over, it's already yesterday's news. Forgotten. Listen. Do you think you could leave tomorrow?'

'Friday? I think so, yes.'

'Good,' she said. 'Because I have a nice surprise for you. Friends of my parents, he's a professor, they have a flat in Hampstead. They're in Canada just now and when I rang my parents the other day they told me I could use the flat any time I want to in the next six weeks. So, I was thinking. Why don't *we* use it? My interview's next Monday. We could leave tomorrow afternoon and have a quiet weekend in London before we both start work.'

'It sounds great.'

'All right, then. Let's plan on it.'

When they reached the BBC on Ormeau Avenue, she hugged

him before getting out of the car. 'Try not to worry,' she said. 'I'll see you tonight.'

He drove back up University Road, passing Queen's, where, on this the last day of graduation, students and their parents again caused traffic jams outside the university gates. He sat, slow in the crawl of cars, and thought of two days ago when he waited with a bomb in his car, the white Ford waiting patiently behind him. And again looked in his rear-view mirror. Was he being followed now? In sudden guilt, he thought of Moira. Was she all right? Where did she spend last night?

At the hotel he went at once to his office and rang the familiar number. Of course, she might not be there. But, on the third ring, he heard her voice. 'Yes?'

'It's me,' he said.

'What do you want?'

'I just wanted to know if you were all right.'

There was a silence on her end of the line. Then she said, 'I spoke to a solicitor this morning. Eamonn McKenna. He'll be in touch with you.'

'About a divorce?'

'That's what you wanted, isn't it?'

'Yes,' he said. 'Look, in the meantime I don't want to see you stuck. I'll put some money in your account today. Are you still going to work for Peg?'

'No, that's off.'

'What do you think you'll do, then?'

'What do you care?'

'Of course I care,' he said. 'You wouldn't think of going back to teaching, would you?'

'What I'm going to do from now on is none of your business. I'm going to do something about the IRA. I'm going to find something, some group, to get me started.'

'Moira,' he said. 'For goodness sake, you can't make a career out of that. Besides, you're not political, you never were.'

'Do you know how many phone calls they got at the studios

after I appeared on telly? You could ask your friend at the BBC. She'll tell you.'

'Look,' he said. 'Getting rid of the IRA – even if you could do it – won't solve the problem. The Protestants here are never going to share jobs and power with the Catholics unless they're forced into it. And the only ones who can force them into it are the British Government. Who haven't got the guts.'

'And who won't have the guts unless we get rid of the IRA first.'

'I see,' he said. 'So Moira Dillon is going to get rid of the IRA?'

'No. But we've got to start something like this. At least, I'm going to try.'

'Well, good luck!'

'Thank you,' she said. 'And good luck to you too.'

He sat at his desk, in a boil of angry thoughts. At least, judging by her past enthusiasms, it won't last more than a month. She hasn't the first idea about how to go about organising a political action group. It's spite, it's getting back at me, it's an effort to make herself into a heroine, with me, the cowardly husband, slinking off to England with his girlfriend. What do I care? What do I care what they think here, I never want to see this place again. Why should I feel guilty about her? Isn't she the one who's putting us at risk?

But at the end of this silent tirade, he felt hollow and ill. If he had not been mixed up with Andrea, would he have been able to persuade Moira to stop this nonsense? With her, he could never be sure. But if anything bad happened to Moira now, he, Andrea – everyone would believe it was his fault.

He looked up. Rory Burke was standing in the doorway. 'Morning,' Rory said. 'Listen, I have a question. Will you be here this afternoon?'

'Yes. Actually, this will be my last day at work. I'm leaving for London tomorrow afternoon.'

'Good. I don't mean good. We're going to miss you. But the

staff wants to give a wee bit of a party for you before you go.'

'No. No, really.'

'You haven't any say in the matter, Michael. I don't think you realise what a big hit you've been here. I know they'll never love me the way they love you.'

'Oh, I'm not sure about that,' he said. 'You're lovable. But, please. No party.'

Of course, he was wasting his breath. At three o'clock that afternoon while he was going over some estimates with McAnally the contractor, Maggie Donlon came in, pinned a carnation on his lapel and led him off to the Dalriada Suite where between fifteen and twenty people were assembled. Drinks were poured and he was toasted. Collis made a speech saying that he had turned the Clarence into a first-class hotel. Mary O'Hara, the assistant housekeeper, burst into tears, telling how he had given her her start. Those staff members who were on duty ducked in and out, keeping the hotel running, but anxious not to miss the party. No one asked him about the bomb or why he was being transferred to London. It was as though he were leaving because of some illness which it was not good manners to talk about. He was one of them, born here like most of them. He understood their way of joking, their way of working, the things they left unsaid. He wondered if he ever again would feel so close to and inspire such affection from people who worked for him. He had left this place and had come back unwillingly, but now, looking at the people around him, hearing the familiar Northern accents, he knew that this was home, that no matter how far his travels, how long his absence, this was the one place where he would not be a stranger, the one place where no one would ever ask, Where are you from? This city, with its ugly streets, its endless rain, its monotonous violence, its Protestant prejudice and Catholic cant and, above all, its copycat English ways, incongruous as a top hat on a Tonga king – all of these things he had wanted to flee now lost their power to anger him. Instead in this crowded room filled with Ulster men and women he felt, as people must have felt in wartime, the fellowship of the besieged. Filled with emotion, he held up his hands for silence and thanked them for the party and for the things they had said. He thanked them for making the Clarence into a first-class hotel. He made a joke, saying that it had taken a bomb to get him out of here and knew from the silence that followed this remark that they did not think of it as a joke at all. He, at once, said awkwardly, 'Well, anyway, God bless, and thanks. Thank you,' and stood back, shy, as they clapped their hands. Collis began to sing, 'For he's a jolly good fellow', and the room filled with singing, the hotel guests staring in at the opened door. Suddenly, he felt he was going to weep. He signalled McAnally, the contractor, who had come in a few minutes earlier, and they left together, people clapping him on the back as he went down the corridor and out to the bomb-damaged site. It had been raining and the sky was cloudy and dull. McAnally's men were clearing off the last of the rubble and, when he looked at the place where he had parked his Renault that morning, the wrecked cars were gone, the parking spaces showed again and on the cracked concrete pavement where his car had been there was his name, 'DILLON', in white painted letters which had somehow survived the explosion.

Next week they would remove his name.

NINE

'It's for you,' Andrea said, coming back into the living-room of her house where he was helping to close her bags.

'Who?'

'I don't know. It's a man's voice.'

In three hours' time they would be on the plane to London. Was it the police? The IRA? His father? 'Sorry,' he said to Andrea. 'But would you mind asking who it is?'

She came back. 'It's a Father Connolly. He says he knows you. He says it's urgent.'

'I don't know any Father Connolly,' he said, but went at once to the phone, nervous. Could something have happened to Moira?

'Yes?' he said.

'Is that you, Mike?' It was a local voice. No one except the Americans called him Mike.

'What is it?'

'This is Matt Connolly, Mike. How are you?'

'I'm sorry. Who?'

'Father Matt. We were at St Michan's together. Now do you remember?'

'Oh, hello,' he said. But the truth was he did not remember.

Most of his schoolmates he had long forgotten. Especially the sort who went on to be priests.

'Listen, Mike. I hear you're taking off for London any time now, is that right?'

'Yes, I'm leaving in an hour or so. What is this about?'

'Mike, it's not something I want to talk about over the phone. Where are you? Could I come up and see you for a wee minute? OK?'

'Look, I'm very busy. What is it? I really have no time.'

'It's important,' the voice said. 'It's not something that can wait. Whereabouts are you?'

He looked at his watch. 'I'm at thirty-one, Mountjoy Avenue. Can you be here in half an hour?'

'Sure, that's only about five minutes away, Mike. I'm at the Clarence. They're the ones who gave me your number. Will I come up?'

'All right.'

He went back into the sitting-room and told Andrea.

'I'll clear out,' she said. 'I have to go down to the office, anyway. Why don't we meet back here at twelve?'

A few minutes after she had gone he stood looking out of the bay window in her sitting-room. A small car drove slowly up the avenue, its occupant searching for house numbers. It went past him, then stopped, backed up, and parked outside his door. A priest got out. He wore dark clerical trousers, a black wind-breaker and a black shirt with a white clerical collar. He was short and stout, about Dillon's age, with thinning hair and a red face. When he had locked the car he turned and stared up at the house. Dillon, standing in the bay window, looked down at him. He looked up at Dillon searchingly, but with no sign of recognition. Then he unlatched the gate, walked up the path, and rang the front doorbell. Dillon went to answer.

When he opened the door the little priest put out his hand tentatively, like a gambler deciding to place his bet. 'Mike, how are you? Remember me now? We were in Senior A together.'

'Come in,' Dillon said. He clasped the priest's hand. It felt wet. He led him into Andrea's sitting-room, its walls embellished with Greenpeace appeals to 'Save the Whales'.

The priest looked at these warily, then pointed to Andrea's luggage which was piled up alongside the coffee table. 'So, you're taking off, are you, Mike? London, is it?'

'Yes.'

The priest, with the confidence of his kind, sat down proprietorially in the best chair and took out cigarettes. 'Smoke? No, I don't blame you. Bad habit.' He grinned up at Dillon, then lit a cigarette. 'Maybe you were the year before me,' he said. 'I have a feeling you don't remember me, Mike?'

'I'm afraid I don't,' Dillon said. 'It was a long time ago.'

'And you went on to Queen's after that, didn't you? And then abroad. The Continent, was it? Or London? Anyway, you don't remember me, but I remember you, well. Wee Matt Connolly? No? Doesn't ring a bell?'

Dillon shook his head and sat down on the window seat, well away from this priest. He looked at the priest's raw, red face, his ice-blue eyes, his confident smile. He knew that 'Wee Father Matt', in the authoritarian way of most Irish priests, thought of himself as someone special, a person of a higher calling than the laymen he dealt with. He would have no idea that, to Dillon, a priest was at best a fool who believed in something totally false, at worst a dangerous meddler in other people's lives.

'No,' he said. 'Wee Matt Connolly? You're right. Doesn't ring a bell.'

'Well, no matter,' the priest said, hitching himself forward in the chair. 'The thing is I've come to ask you a favour. Well, not a favour, exactly. There's something I want to discuss with you. It concerns a boy I know. Actually, he's the son of a parishioner of mine, a lovely woman, I won't give you her name, you'll see why in a minute.' The priest then looked around as though worried that they might be overheard. He leaned forward even further, sitting now on the edge of the armchair, lowering his voice to a confessional murmur. 'It's to do with this business the other night, with yourself and your wife. Can I ask you one thing? Are you going to England for good?'

'Why do you want to know?'

It was as though with that question Dillon had declared his hostility. At once the priest's confidence seemed to falter. 'Sorry, now; it's none of my business, of course. I just wondered.'

'Wondered what?'

'I wondered if it had anything to do with – you know, being worried about the Rah.'

'The what?'

'The Rah, the I R A – you know, that's what people call them.'

'You mean that's what their supporters call them?'

The priest tried a smile. 'Mike, I'm sure I know how you feel, people breaking into your house at night, pulling guns on you and your wife. Who could blame you? But, the thing is, nobody was hurt. Thanks to you, of course. Now, I know that Mrs Dillon is very much against the Rah. She's taking a strong line. Now, it seems she told some newspaper people that you recognised one of these lads who came to your house?'

'Where did you see that?' Dillon asked. 'It wasn't in the papers, was it?'

'I don't know,' the priest said. 'Maybe not. Anyway, I heard it somewhere. Or maybe it was the police that said it, when they came to see her. They came to lift her son.'

'And did they "lift" him?'

'No. He wasn't at home.'

'Was he one of the ones who were in our house that night?'

'Oh, no, Mike,' the priest said. 'Take it easy, now. I'm not saying that. The trouble is, this boy is very headstrong and his mother thinks he just *might* be mixed up with the Rah. When the police came round he wasn't home, as I said. And the truth is, she hasn't seen him since. Poor woman, she's half demented, worrying about him.'

'Is his name Kev?'

There was a silence. The priest's red face flushed full of blood, his icy blue eyes blinked as though faced by a bright light. 'Kev,' he said, neither affirming nor questioning the name, pronouncing it as though it were a foreign word he had just learned. 'This woman's a lovely woman,' he said. 'She only has the one child. The father died ten years ago. You know what these lads are like, they're just kids. They get these romantic notions. They see the injustice around them. Die for Ireland. All that. We heard it all in school.'

'Yes, we did,' Dillon said. 'That was one of the troubles with our school.'

'Depends on your point of view,' the priest said. 'There *is* injustice here. Discrimination against Catholics is a terrible thing. These kids see that.'

'We all see that,' Dillon said. 'But does that justify going into someone's house at night and threatening to kill his wife if he doesn't go out and plant a bomb in a place where a whole lot of innocent people will be killed? What's the Fifth Commandment, Father? "Thou shalt not kill".'

'Hold on now, Mike,' the priest said, an edge of anger in his voice. 'I take your point. I'm not saying I agree with these kids. I say they see what's going on here as a political situation. There *is* injustice here. You know that as well as I do. This boy I'm talking about, he's only nineteen. He's not a murderer or a criminal. Maybe he's misguided, I'll grant you that. But we're talking about him being locked up in a place like Long Kesh for maybe as long as fifteen years. That's shocking waste of a young life. And I'm thinking of his mother, too. Of her life from now on, if that happens.'

'And what about my wife?' Dillon said. 'What if they'd killed her?'

'Ah, but they didn't, did they?' the priest said. 'They probably had no intention. I mean, they left the house before it was time for the bomb to go off. I mean, there you are.'

'But they did intend to kill Pottinger. And if that meant

blowing up whatever poor souls happened to be in the same building as him, that was all right, too. I'll tell you something, *Father*. If the police find that boy, Kev – vicious little bastard that he is – I'll make sure he's a lot older before he gets a chance to kill anybody else.'

When he had said it he sat, staring at the priest's red face, knowing at last what he had done. It had been said. It was as clear as if he had said it to the IRA themselves.

'Well, of course, that's up to you, Mike,' the priest said. 'I can see you're very angry about this. I quite understand. But, just let me say that if I was you I'd think about it. You're off to England now. It may never come up. I sincerely hope it doesn't. But, considering the – political climate here . . . well, sometimes it's not a good idea to get too involved. You know what I mean. My problem now is, what will I tell his mother? I wouldn't like to tell her what you just said. She's worried enough as it is.'

'Tell her what you like,' Dillon said, standing up.

The priest stood up too. There was a silence. 'Well, thanks for seeing me, anyway,' the priest said, and this time he did not offer his hand.

He walked ahead of the priest into the hall. He opened the front door to let him out. He had said it. It was too late to take it back. He watched the short, stout figure go down the path. At the gate, after opening it, the priest turned and looked back at him. 'Think about it, will you?' he said. 'Bye, now. Safe journey.'

The priest walked to his car, unlocked the door and got in. The little car turned around in the street and went back the way it had come.

'Are you worried about it?' Andrea said later. 'You are, aren't you?'

'I should have kept my mouth shut.'

159

'Anyway, the police haven't found him. He's probably down South by now.'

'Maybe. But what if they pick him up in six months' or a year's time? It will always be hanging over my head, damn it.'

They were outside her house, putting her bags and his into the rented car for the drive to the airport. 'Wait,' she said. 'Is that everything?' She went up the path to the front door and turned to look back at him, smiling, holding up her key for him to see, then posting it back through the letterbox. She came down the path, shut the gate and said, 'That's it. Goodbye, Belfast. We're on our way.'

They drove up Peter's Hill, along the Shankill Road, the working-class Protestant ghetto. Within minutes they had left the city and were driving along the hedged country roads which had not changed since his childhood. It was a clear Irish summer's day, white clouds lazy in blue skies, a cool breeze, sunlight on the rolling hills above the lough. As they approached the airport, police were flagging down cars and trucks, moving them into a roadside detour to search for hidden guns and bombs. But, as they drove up to this checkpoint, the armed, flak-jacketed policeman in their path peered in at them through the car's windshield, then, straightening up, waved them on through, unsearched. Dillon, seeing the airport terminal ahead, thought of old wartime films, the car passing through a frontier station, the border guards waving the escapees on to freedom. There was one last link with the past, one thing he had not done. When the car stopped at the terminal entrance he said to Andrea, 'I have to make a phone call. Would you mind turning in the car?'

He loaded the baggage on to a metal trolley and watched as she drove off to the Avis car-park. He pushed the trolley into the terminal building, searching for a public phone. When he found one he rang Donegal.

'Is that you, Mister Michael?' It was Deirdre's voice. 'She's up in the vegetable garden. Will you wait till I fetch her, or do you want her to ring you back?'

'I'll wait.'

Opposite him was an airport gift shop, with racks of magazines, paperback books, gimcrack gifts, children's toys. He stood staring at them, his mind far away, in the gravelled walk behind Kinsallagh House, seeing her come out of the walled vegetable garden, her old blue gardening hat pulled down over her lank grey hair, wearing a rain jacket greened with age, worn wellies and a tweed skirt, long out of style. She would be pulling off her gardening gloves and putting them in the trug which she carried like a handbag. Tall, thin, she still had the walk of a young girl, a girl now faded into a grey, often silent figure who, nevertheless, was the true owner of the hotel and its grounds.

It had always been the same: his father meeting the guests, peacocking in the public rooms; his mother shy, behind the scenes, buying supplies, running the staff, supervising the meals, and, in the time she stole from these busy hours, walking, solitary, in her gardens, devoted as a priestess in some sacred grove, feeding, planting, pruning, giving the gardens colour and life. His mother was at home in Kinsallagh as his father would never be. She had been born in a large country house in County Cork. Her father, a minister in the first Irish government, retired there to farm and practise law when De Valera came to power. Dillon's mother, born and brought up in an Ireland free from British rule, had in the eleven years she lived in Belfast, those first eleven years of her son's life, remained a stranger to the North. She was, he sometimes thought, a typical Southerner in her attitude to Ulster. To her it was a separate place, a place left behind when Ireland formed itself into a small nation state with its own flag, its own currency, its government, police and army, its delegates to international councils, its peacekeeping forces in the Middle East, its street signs and official documents in a language few people understood. In fifty years of separation, North and South had become alien to each other as never in the centuries of English rule. The Southern Irish did not brood on Ulster's troubles. They had troubles of their own. The North was another country, ruled by Britain. It was a place they did not quite understand.

Now, holding the receiver to his ear, he heard her footsteps in that faraway hall, heard her soft Southern voice say, 'Mary, the creamery milk is here. Will you tell Pat?' And then, calm as though she had not been worried, she picked up the phone and said, 'Is it you? I hear you're off to England, is that right?'

'I'm at the airport now. I meant to ring you sooner.'

'Don't worry. I know you were very busy. Your father told me. What a terrible business that was.'

'Yes . . . Anyway, it's over now.'

'Is it?' she said. 'Good. How's Moira?'

'She's all right. At least I hope she is. I wanted to tell you. She's not coming with me.'

'Why not?'

'She doesn't think we should leave. She wants to stay here.'

'Oh,' his mother said in that quiet voice she used as a shield to hide her thoughts. 'Does that mean you're breaking up with her?'

'Yes. Actually, it started before all this. It – it would have happened anyway.'

'Well, I can't say I'm surprised,' his mother said.

He was surprised that she had said it. 'Why is that?' he asked.

'Well, you weren't very happy together, were you? I had that impression. Your father and I don't agree on this, but I never thought Moira was very stable, poor girl. Are you going to get a divorce?'

His mother was religious as his father was not. For her, divorce must seem a grave sin.

'I have to,' he said. 'There's someone else.'

'An Irish girl?'

'No, she's Canadian.'

'But you'd live in England?'

'Yes.'

He heard her catch her breath and then she said, 'Your father doesn't know any of this, does he?'

'No. I wanted to talk to you first.'

'I'll tell him,' she said. 'Michael?'

'Yes?'

'Are you sure this time? About this girl?'

'Yes, Mama, I'm sure.'

'Is she worried, the girl? I mean about the IRA?'

'Not as much as I am,' he said. 'That's why we're going to live in England.'

'That's not the real reason,' his mother said. 'You always wanted to get away from here, didn't you? Still, I suppose it's the best thing. That's what the police advised, isn't it?'

'Yes. Mama, I have to go now.'

'I know. Michael, I'm glad you rang. I'm glad you told me. And good luck with the new job. The Ormonde, is it?'

'Yes.'

'I'll keep in touch with Moira,' his mother said. 'I think I should, don't you?'

'Yes. I'm worried about her.'

'I know. Anyway, good luck again. What's your girl's name?'

'Andrea.'

'Andrea,' his mother said, testing it out. 'Well, my love to both of you.'

'Goodbye, Mama. I'll ring you from London.'

When he put the receiver down he saw Andrea waiting by the luggage trolley. 'All set?' she asked.

'Yes. That was my mother.'

'Oh.' She turned the trolley towards the ramp which led to the departure area. 'What's she like?'

'She sends you her love,' he said. 'That's what she's like.'

Andrea laughed, pleased and embarrassed. 'That sounds promising. You're very fond of her, aren't you?'

He nodded. 'Yes. But I don't know her.'

He took the trolley and began to push it up the ramp towards the ticket counters. There seemed to be extra police on duty. Four of them stood by the baggage detection devices, watching as travellers' hand luggage was passed through. The shuttle was due to leave in twenty minutes and as he finished ticketing and went through the security check, he could see the British Airways plane waiting on the runway. Cleared through security, they were now in a lounge for passengers only.

Four policemen came into the lounge escorting a man in a blue pinstripe suit. The man carried an official-looking brief-case. The airline staff on the departure gate opened the gate and the man, accompanied by the police, went out of the building, walked across the tarmac, and went, solitary, up the steps of the ladder leading to the waiting plane.

The police came back into the lounge. 'Some bigshot,' Andrea said. 'British, I guess.'

Suddenly, he wished he were like that special passenger, already safely on the plane. The four policemen, laughing and talking as though their job were done, went over to the small bar and ordered cups of tea. He was glad the police were close. He looked at the other people in the lounge. Was there someone watching him, someone who would get on the phone once the plane took off? But then he thought of his visitor this morning, saw the priest's red face and uneasy smile. They would already know that he was going to England. They would know he had promised to identify Kev. Sooner or later, they would discover that he was working at the Ormonde. They would find him there.

Yet, when the flight was called and he boarded with Andrea and sat, looking down on the green Antrim hills and the sweep of the lough as the plane began its climb, he felt again the elation of escape. The plane turned towards the Irish sea, the shoreline reeling away at an angle, and now he saw only the illimitable grey anonymity of ocean, and, far below, a solitary ship, tiny as a toy.

Drinks were served. He sat, holding Andrea's hand, waiting

for that other coast to appear. When it did and they were over England, he looked down at the well-kept fields, the busy roads, the towns meshing into suburbs which soon became more towns. Already Ireland seemed a small empty island, lost in the shadow of this land with its millions of people and its history linked to a larger world. He was going back now to that larger world. He had ended a part of his life, his marriage to Moira, his work at the Clarence, his stay in Belfast. With Andrea he was beginning something new. Don't think about Kev, about the priest, about any of that. It's over.

An hour later he stood in Heathrow terminal watching the Ulster passengers collect their luggage and move off into the crowd, swallowed up in this kaleidoscope of different sights and sounds. He and Andrea found a taxi and drove to the Hampstead address where her friends had their flat. It was on the upper floor of a large Victorian house in a street just off Primrose Hill. The flat itself was large with a drawing-room filled with paintings and books, many of them familiar volumes of poetry and fiction by writers whose work he admired. The house was in a quiet street and outside the front window a large oak tree reared up incongruously from the small patch of yard. It was the sort of London flat he had always wanted to have and being in it now gave him a feeling of pleasure and security.

'How long did you say we could stay in this place?' he asked Andrea, lifting her up and whirling her around in the hallway.

'Six weeks. I think they're coming back at the end of August. It's nice, isn't it?'

'It's great. They must be rich.'

'No, they're Canadian academics. He's from Montreal. Why did you think they were rich?'

'Because no professor I know could afford a flat like this as a *pied-à-terre*.'

'Really? I never thought of that. They're people like my parents. I suppose it's different in Canada.'

How different was it? he wondered later as they walked up

Primrose Hill. People like her parents. Her father was an engineer with his own consulting firm. He was probably the sort who wouldn't be very keen on his daughter marrying the lowly assistant manager of a London hotel. He had not thought of Andrea as rich. In Belfast she had lived like a student, the attic room, the second-hand bed, the broken-down furniture, the flat shared with three other girls. But what if she were the child of rich parents, used to comforts he could not provide? And in London, working for the BBC, she would become part of the intellectual establishment, entering a world he had once hoped to join. Would she be ashamed of him?

'By the way,' he said. 'I think it would be a good idea if we don't mention this IRA thing or what I'm doing here. I mean, to people we meet in London.'

'Yes, I suppose so,' she said, but she did not seem to be listening. They had reached the lookout on top of the hill. She pointed to the London skyline, blurred and distant in the afternoon haze. 'Isn't that the Post Office tower?'

'Yes, that's it. The funny thing sticking up there.'

'Aren't you excited?' she said. 'Living here? Of course, I forgot. You lived here before. This is where you met Moira, isn't it?'

'Yes. She didn't like London.'

'Do you know, I sort of hate her now,' Andrea said. 'If anything happens to you, it will be her fault. I think if it did I'd go back and kill her.'

'Nothing's going to happen,' he said.

On the slopes below them people were exercising their dogs in the English manner, letting the dogs off the lead, the dogs running to meet and sniff at other dogs, the owners walking on, confident that, when they called, the dogs would come to heel. It was a scene pastoral as an eighteenth-century painting: the park, like all of London's parks, open and serene, a place where people walked unafraid, shutting the city out. He turned to her. 'Tomorrow, let's get some food and come here for a picnic.'

166

'Oh, listen,' she said. 'I forgot to tell you. Elsa Taylor, she's a friend of mine, she's arranged a little party for tomorrow evening, a sort of welcome-to-London thing. It's for us.'

'What sort of party? I mean, who'll be there?'

'I don't know. People I'll be working with, I guess. BBC types.'

'What do *you* do?' he said, putting on a plummy English accent. 'I work in a hotel. Do you, indeed? Hmm.'

'Oh, darling,' she said. 'Stop worrying about things that don't matter.'

'But it does matter. Now that I'm with you, I wish I had a job I liked better.'

She looked at him strangely, he thought, as though he had said something she didn't expect.

'Well, if you want to change jobs, it's not too late, is it?' she said. 'Look at the changes you've made in the past week. Listen, we're together. That's what matters, isn't it? I'm happy. Aren't you?'

He kissed her then, on Primrose Hill, high over London, and, as he did, her happiness flowed into him like a current. She was right. They were here. Everything had changed. Everything.

The party on Saturday evening was held in an ugly block of flats on the edge of Camden Town. Andrea suggested that they bring something, so he arrived at Elsa Taylor's door carrying two bottles of wine in a brown paper bag, almost dropping them when Elsa, a very pretty girl in her twenties, hugged him, saying, 'So you're Michael. Welcome to London. This party's for you, you know.'

The narrow entrance hall was already crowded with people and the people seemed young, noisy and untidy, not at all the sort who would give a damn what he did for a living. As Elsa led them around introducing them he began to enjoy himself as though, mysteriously, he had been transported back to his student days. Andrea, who did not know the people either, kept close to him and put her arm around him as they were drawn into conversations about films, ecological disaster, new books, most of it dealt with by hyperbole and jokes. There was food laid out on a table, and later, a little drunk, they sat in the bedroom with Elsa, eating pizza from paper plates. When they had finished, he and Andrea went out on to a narrow back balcony. Below, in an empty site, a huge hole was being dug to lay the foundations of a building.

'Great view,' he said. 'Looks like a bombsite.'

Suddenly, she turned to him, holding him, pressing her body against his. 'Are you all right?'

'Yes, of course,' he said. 'I'm having a great time. What about you?'

She looked back inside. The crowd was thinning out. 'Yes. Elsa's really nice, isn't she? But listen. Let's go home now.'

Twenty minutes later as they went up Haverstock Hill, he saw two policemen coming towards them, walking their beat. In their white summer shirts and old-fashioned helmets, they seemed young, innocent, unthreatening, no kin to the Ulster police. He realised then that for the past twenty-four hours he had not thought of the Chief Inspector, the priest, the voice on the phone. Was it over? Was it possible, here in London, to slip back into the safe anonymous river of ordinary life?

On Sunday morning they slept late. When they woke the street was quiet and birds chirped under the roof above their bedroom window. They made coffee, dressed, and walked up to the high street where they bought the Sunday papers and carried them to the park. They sat under a tree, reading in desultory fashion, then lay down together, side by side. He held her hand as they looked up at the empty summer sky. A squirrel ran up to them, stood on its hind legs, stared, then dropped down and scuttled off. Somewhere in the distance a clock struck twelve. She told him about Sundays in Toronto when she was a little girl: how her parents would take her for walks in an area of ravines which were, improbably, near the centre of the city; how in summer they would sail on a lake and in winter skate on a pond. It seemed far away and in the past but, looking at her, he could see what she must have been like as that little girl. At one, they went and had lunch in the garden of a Hampstead pub and later walked down through Regent's Park into the shut Sunday streets of the West End. Andrea did not know London as he did. He became her guide. They walked and walked, until they had reached Chelsea and the river. As they strolled along the Embankment the sky darkened. A sudden rain came down, drenching the streets. They sheltered in a shop doorway and, when he saw a taxi with its light lit, he ran out in the downpour, waving. In the taxi, going home from the long walk, wet from the rain, he sat with his arm around her, dulled with contentment.

That morning before going out they had closed all the windows in the flat. Returning, they found the rooms hot and airless. He went into the drawing-room and opened the floor-length windows which looked down on the street. The rain had stopped. He could hear the tick of the grandfather clock in the passageway leading to the bedroom. She went into the bedroom and came out, drying her hair with a large white towel. She had taken off her wet dress and wore only a pair of blue cotton panties. She came into the drawing-room and lay down on the long sofa. He looked at her, then went into the bedroom, stripped off his wet clothes, and came back naked to the drawing-room. Cool damp air flowed through the open windows. She lay on the sofa, looking up at him, seeing that he was aroused. He sat on the sofa and stroked her breasts and thighs, then, pulling down her blue panties, he eased them off her ankles. They began to make love.

Later, as they lay on the carpet holding each other, looking up at the sky through the opened windows, the rain began again. Large drops, almost like hailstones, spattered into the room. He got up, closed the windows, and came back to her. Again, they made love. The rain stopped and, as they lay quiet in the room, the day dying, the sky turning dark, the grandfather clock ticking steady as a heartbeat, he turned to her. He wanted to say to her that he had never been so happy, that today was the happiest day in his whole life. But did it need to be said, or would saying it break the day's spell? He kissed her instead.

At nine o'clock he went out alone, and walked, searching until he found a little Indian-run grocery where he bought bread, cold meat, potato salad, beer and a runny looking chocolate cake. He came back to the flat, ducking into doorways to avoid the showers. When he rang the doorbell she came down to let him in. She was wearing a cotton frock, pale-grey with pink stripes, looking very different from her usual jeans-and-blouse self. He thought what it would be like to come home to her every evening. He thought of their new life here in London. He thought of last night's party and of the friends they would make, the concerts, the exhibitions they would go to, the trips they would take to Paris, Venice, Normandy and Provence. As they sat in the kitchen eating the food he had bought, they talked of these things. Then, suddenly weary from the long day's walking, the lovemaking, the open air, they were sleepy, wanting bed. In the bedroom she fell asleep in his arms. He lay holding her, fighting his own drowsiness. It was like a time long ago, the time of his childhood. He did not want to close his eyes. He did not want this day to end.

TEN

'Of course I remember you,' Ronny Pomfret said. But Dillon knew he did not. When he had worked for Ronny nine years ago at the Ormonde he had been a lowly trainee just out of hotel school. Now, things were different. Ronny was receiving him in his private office at ten in the morning, had ordered coffee, and discussed the recent events in Belfast as though he and Dillon were equals in the Alliance hotel hierarchy. Again, he wondered if Ronny, who was close to retirement, was looking him over as a potential successor. But, almost as if he had spoken the thought, Ronny smiled at him and said, 'Of course, being here is just a stopgap for you, isn't it?'

'Is it? I don't know what the plans are.'

'Well, I don't have to tell you, they're delighted at the way you turned things around at the Clarence. And between ourselves I think you're going to be asked to do something similar again. Do you know a hotel called the Wellington? It's in South Ken.'

He did know the Wellington. It had once been very well known indeed. 'But it's not ours,' he said.

'The rumour is, Dan Keogh is just about to buy it,' Ronny Pomfret said. 'And I wouldn't be at all surprised if they wanted something similar to the job you did on the Clarence. On a grander scale, of course. Mind you, officially, I know nothing.'

'Of course.'

'Well, there it is,' Ronny said. 'Just remember to be surprised if Dan brings it up. Meanwhile, I'm delighted to have you back here. Let's go down now and I'll introduce you to Johnny Harper. You'll be taking over from him for the next few weeks.'

An hour later, walking through the Ormonde's baroque public rooms with Harper who was soon to go on leave, Dillon felt both elated and confused. Yesterday he had wanted to change his job. But if he had been asked what he would have liked to do in London, provided he stayed in the business, it would have been to make over and run some famous old hotel. Here in the Ormonde, even if one day he should inherit Ronny's job, he would be part of something which did not need changing, a hotel too large to be under one man's control. But the Wellington was of medium size, a place which had once been very grand, with a history of guests who were part of history. Did he really want to look for a job outside the hotel business? What did he know of other jobs when he had trained and spent his whole working life in this one? Remembering the pleasures of the weekend just ended he again felt a rush of hope. Was this the turning point he had so often dreamed of, the end of useless daydreams, of nostalgia for his student days, of that failed hope of writing poetry which, in Belfast, had been signposted for him daily in those familiar, remembered, unloved streets?

That morning Andrea had gone to the BBC in Portland Place to meet the people she would work with. He had arranged to telephone her after lunch. At three o'clock he rang her. 'How did it go?'

'Great,' she said. 'I'm pleased. It's going to be an interesting job. And you, how was it?'

'I shouldn't tell you this,' he said. But he did, he told her about the Wellington.

'You sound happy about it.'

'I am. I mean, if I'm not going to change jobs, this is as good a chance as I'm likely to get. Listen, when are you finishing today?'

'I don't know. I haven't really started work yet. I guess I'm free any time.'

'Let's meet at five,' he said. 'Here at the Ormonde. We'll have a drink and then maybe we'll snoop over to have a look at the Wellington. All right?'

'At five, then.'

'Ask for me at the desk,' he said. 'I'll be looking out for you.'

At four, having taken leave of Harper, he was free to go home. Instead, he went across the street for a walk in Hyde Park, and, at five, returned to the Ormonde to meet her. He looked around in the lobby and in the main lounges but she was not there. He then went to ask at reception and as he passed the concierge's desk he saw her come out of a nearby cloakroom. As always, his heart raced. He went to her and kissed her. 'It *is* grand,' she said. 'It's also enormous.'

'But boring,' he said. 'Wait till you see the Wellington. Come, let's have a drink!'

He led her into the large art deco bar which was just off the main lobby. As he did, one of the porters came up to him, handing him a telephone message slip. 'We paged you, sir, but we must have missed you. We thought you'd gone home.'

He read the slip. 'Something wrong?' Andrea asked. He gave her the slip which read *Please call Detective Inspector Randall*. There was a telephone number with a Belfast prefix.

'Who is he?'

'Special Branch. His boss is the head of the anti-terrorist squad.'

She looked at him. 'What do you think it is?'

'I don't know. Let me get you a drink and then I'll find out.'

The bar was already filling up for the cocktail hour. As he signalled a waiter and ordered drinks he felt the same tremor in his body as he had felt driving towards the Clarence with a bomb in his car. He did not want her to see his agitation, but she looked at him and at once put her hand on his sleeve. 'Are you all right, Michael? Have a drink. You can phone him later.' He shook his head, smiled at her, then went out into the main lobby. He did not want to phone from the hotel's administrative offices. It was not a conversation for others to overhear. He went across the lobby and saw that there were three pay telephone booths beside the main cloakroom. One of them was free. He went in and used a phone card.

'Detective Inspector Randall, please.'

'Who's calling?'

'My name is Michael Dillon. I'm returning his call.'

Almost as though he were on the other line, Randall said, 'That you, Mr Dillon? Randall speaking. How's the weather in London?'

'It's sunny.'

'Ah, you're lucky. You know, it's a fact that the weather's always better in London than it is here. Did you have a good weekend, then?'

'Yes, thanks. What did you ring me about?'

'Well, I'm calling about a young man called Kevin McDowell. We picked him up over the weekend. I have a feeling he might be one of the ones we're looking for.'

At the cloakroom next to the booth Dillon was standing in, a uniformed porter was handing a gentleman his umbrella. Simultaneously, the head porter came out of the cloakroom, nodding to the gentleman, then going on out into the main lobby. The head porter, a dignified figure wearing a top hat with a thick gold band around it and a frockcoat with gold arm-facings, had been introduced to Dillon earlier that day. Now, seeing Dillon in the telephone booth, the head porter smiled at him and tipped his index finger to the rim of his hat in a respectful, but jovial, salute.

'Hello?' said Randall's voice, back in Belfast.

'Sorry. You were saying?'

'Well, if he's the one you saw that night, we'd have a very good start. What I'm asking is, could you come and have a look at him? I mean, you could come over and go back on the same day.'

'Well, I've just started work here,' Dillon said. 'I'm going to be very busy for the next day or two.'

'Maybe towards the middle of the week, then? We'd bring you over and send you back, of course. And you wouldn't have to worry. Nobody would know you'd been here.'

'Have you told my wife about this?'

'No, not yet. After all, you were the one who saw his face.'

'Well, don't mention it to her, will you? I'd rather you didn't worry her just now. She's quite highly strung.'

'Yes, right. So, when do you think – Wednesday or Thursday? I mean, if he's not the right man, we don't want to hold him any longer than necessary.'

'Look. I'll have to speak to my bosses here.'

'Of course, of course. Maybe after you've spoken to them you can give me a shout?'

'All right.'

'Thanks, Mr Dillon. Oh, by the way, I don't have your phone number. Do you have one?'

'It's nine three five six eight four one.'

'Right. Thanks again. So I'll expect your call tomorrow morning, then? Is that OK?'

'Yes.'

He put the receiver down and stood in the telephone booth, looking out at the porters, the lobby, the people coming into the hotel through the revolving doors. He saw them hesitate in the moment of coming out of the moving doors, saw them look about, choose a direction and move off towards it. An elderly

175

man with a rose in his buttonhole embraced a middle-aged lady who had hurried to greet him. A man in a tan suit, entering the lobby, looked around, then waved to a stout man who sat in a lobby armchair, a white panama hat resting on his knees. It was like a scene in a film. He was not part of this film. It was not part of his life.

When he went back into the hotel bar he saw Andrea turn anxiously in his direction. 'Well?' she asked.

He sat down. He had ordered a gin and tonic and now he drank some of it. 'Tell me,' she said. 'What is it? Is it something about Moira?'

He told her. As he spoke, he could hear the murmurs of other conversations, the faint noise of glasses being placed on tables, distant laughter from the area around the bar. He heard these things at a remove as though he had gone slightly deaf. His voice, telling her, seemed to be the voice of some person other than himself.

When he had finished, she reached across the table and put her hand on his. '*Don't*,' she said.

'What do you mean?'

'Don't do it. Why should you? You've done enough. You told the police when it really mattered – when you had a bomb in your car. But this is different. If you identify this Kev, it will be like putting out a contract on your own life. Moira's the one who wants to fight the IRA and make herself a hero. OK, let her do it. But why you? Didn't you once tell me enough people have died for Ireland? Not that you'd even be dying for Ireland. You'd just be a statistic in this mess. And what about us?'

She was crying. He looked at her and knew that what she said was right. That it was what he wanted her to say, wanted someone to say.

'Wait,' he said. 'Don't cry. You're right. The other day when I told the priest I'd identify that kid, I was being stupid. Because the important thing is us. Not keeping the police happy. Not getting back at the IRA. The minute we got out of Northern

Ireland I saw this thing for what it was. A moronic bloody mess. To hell with it.'

'Do you mean it?'

'Of course I mean it.'

'Oh, my God,' she said. 'Michael, that's great.'

'So, it's settled then,' he said. 'I'll ring him in the morning. What should I say?'

'Just say you don't want to do it. Say you're not really sure you saw his face. Say anything. They'll get the message. People don't testify against the IRA. The police are used to it.'

'But what about Moira? What if they try her next?'

'But she didn't see him, did she?' Andrea said. 'The police know that. Come on, let's have another drink. I'm shaking. You'd think it was me they'd phoned.'

He signalled to a waiter. The voices of people at the tables around him became louder as though his deafness had cleared. If he refused to testify, the news would quickly get back to the kitchen of some row house on the Falls Road, or a cellblock in Long Kesh prison. There, the ones who made the decisions to kill informers would know that fear had made him hold his tongue. The priest would believe that his warning had been heeded. The police would have to release Kev for lack of evidence. The IRA would not bother with Moira. She knew nothing, she was just some woman talking out against them and the IRA did not heed women. He was their target: he had always been their target. They were already planning other murders, other bombings. Tomorrow, when he told the police, it would be over.

The waiter brought them their second drink. Lightheaded with relief, he began to tell Andrea what he knew about the Wellington Hotel: how it had been the favourite hotel of Eastern potentates, at the time of the Great Exhibition of 1851; how Oscar Wilde had been booed and spat upon when he spoke at a banquet there; how the main dining-room was celebrated for its extravagant murals painted by the Spanish artist José Maria

Sert who had stayed there in the twenties with Diaghilev and Serge Lifar.

Andrea, listening, laughed and made fun of his enthusiasm for the hotel's artistic links and, when he had signed for the drinks, they took the tube up to Hampstead and ate dinner in a little Greek taverna, a few streets from their flat. Not once, in the entire evening, did either of them mention the police or the past. It was not until they lay together in the dark, listening to the tick of the grandfather clock in the hall, that she said, 'Why don't you ring them before you go to work? That way, we'll have it over with.'

'All right.'

She held him then, kissing him. 'Let's go away somewhere next weekend,' she said. 'Somewhere in the country.'

'Good.'

She slept. He did not. Tomorrow morning he would make the telephone call. It was the right thing to do. It was the only thing to do. By making the phone call he was protecting Andrea as well as himself. By making it he was also protecting Moira, mad Moira with her idea of an anti-IRA crusade. By making the phone call he would put an end to all of this. It was an accident that he had been the manager of the Clarence at a time when the IRA was planning to murder one of its enemies. It had nothing to do with him.

He did not sleep. He lay, hour after hour, in the suburban stillness of the night. If he had agreed to co-operate what good would it have done? The IRA would still break into people's homes, and terrorise them, and use them to help carry out their murder plans. Because people, ordinary people, would always be afraid. And people, ordinary people, would be sensible and see that their lives were more important than whether Catholics in Northern Ireland were given their fair share of jobs and votes. It did not matter one jot in the history of the world whether Ireland became united. Northern Ireland was not an occupied country like France under the Nazis. The majority of its people wanted it to remain as part of Great Britain. There was no reason to go on risking his life.

But, there, in the dark, those arguments raced in his mind, angry, declamatory, as though he had been accused. By phoning the police tomorrow and refusing to testify, he would be admitting that he was afraid, that, again, the IRA had won.

Outside, in the avenue, in the first light of day, he heard the sound of birds waking, beginning their territorial calls. And at last, weary, he fell asleep. When he woke an hour later it was to the sound of a telephone ringing.

Andrea had already got out of bed and gone into the hall to answer it. He heard her speak. 'Yes, he's here. Who's calling? Hold on, please.'

She came back into the bedroom. 'It's Moira.'

At once he felt his heart thump. 'What's happened?'

'She wants to speak to you.'

Naked, he ran into the hall and picked up the phone. 'Hello?'

'Sorry to disturb you,' she said. 'The Ormonde gave me this number.'

'That's all right. What's up? Are you OK?'

'Yes, I suppose so. I'm calling you because I had a visitor last night.'

'Who?' he said, and heard the tremor in his voice.

'A priest. A Father Matt Connolly. He says he was at school with you.'

Relief made him lean back against the wall and catch his breath. 'What did he want?'

'He says the police have lifted his nephew.'

'His *nephew?*'

'Yes. Kevin McDowell is his name. It sounds as if he's the Kev – the awful one, do you remember?'

'Yes.'

'Anyway, this priest said he'd spoken to you before you left and you told him that if you could identify any of those IRA, you bloody well would. Is that true?'

179

'Yes, I did.'

'He was in a panic. He wanted me to stop you. Now that they've found this wee bugger he knows you could put him away for a good few years.'

'What did you say to him?'

'I said if my husband would do that, then I certainly wouldn't try to stop him. Michael?'

He waited. She did not speak for a moment and then he realised that she had begun to weep. 'What is it?' he said. 'What's wrong?'

'He said the IRA knew you saw Kev's face. They know you're going to testify. He says he doesn't want to see you killed. He was in a state, I tell you. But he made me mad. He's an irritating wee sort, isn't he?'

'Yes, I know.'

'Anyway, I sent him away. Then I lay awake all night thinking. And in the middle of the night I realised that, when you phoned the police that morning, it wasn't because you wanted to get rid of me – '

'Of course it wasn't!'

'All right, all right,' she said crossly. 'I just said I was wrong. You did it because you thought it was the right thing to do. And now you're going to do it again. But, Michael, listen. What Mama said is right. It's just madness. It's not worth it. And in the middle of the night I thought: He's doing this because he wants to show he's not afraid, the way I said he was. Listen, don't heed what I said. It was wrong. If anything happens to you now, I'll have to live with it for the rest of my life. And I don't want that. Do you hear me, Michael?'

'That goes for both of us,' he said. 'I don't want anything happening to you, either. Now, listen to me. I'm going to call the police this morning. I'm not going to testify. It's a pity to let those bastards get away with it, but still . . . '

'Oh, God.' He heard her catch her breath. 'Listen, do it now, will you? And, listen, that Father Connolly wanted to know where he could reach you in London. Of course, I didn't tell him. Look – he's in with the IRA, I'm sure he is. Is there any way you can reach him? He'll pass the word on to them.'

'Don't worry,' he said. 'Everything's going to be all right.'

'Is it?' she said. 'Michael?'

'What?'

'Listen, I want to ask you something. I've been thinking. Was it my fault or yours? I mean, did you ever love me? It wasn't *just* my looks, was it?'

'No,' he said. 'No, it wasn't.'

'You did like me, didn't you?'

'I still do.'

'Well . . . ' She was silent and then said, 'I'll say goodbye now. And don't forget. Ring them up right away.'

'I will. Take care of yourself, Moira.'

'Goodbye, then,' she said again.

Andrea, wearing her pink-and-grey dress, stood at the bedroom door, looking out at him. 'What was all that about?'

He told her. 'That priest worries me,' she said. 'If he's scared, then you should be too.'

'What do you mean?'

'Look, I'll make some coffee. It's only seven. Is it too early to ring the Inspector?'

'I think so.'

'Well, call him anyway. Try?'

'I'll wait till eight,' he said.

They went together into the kitchen. He was thinking of Moira. He went to the window. Sunlight filtered through the leafy branches of the oak tree outside. 'Look,' he said. 'It's a lovely morning.'

'Is it?'

'Now, stop that.' He went to her and kissed her.

'Is there any way you can get in touch with the priest?'

'I could ring around, I suppose. Look, it's all right. We're in London. They don't know where I am.'

'He told them you'd testify. They'll listen to him.'

'Make the coffee,' he said. 'I'll make the toast.'

'Ring the police. Please? Now?'

'All right.'

He went back into the bedroom and found the special telephone number Randall had given him. He looked again at the bed where he had lain awake for most of the night, thinking of this moment, this call. In a shutter flash of memory, in the mirror of the front room in Winchester Avenue Kev lifted his woollen mask and scratched the sore under his left eye: he saw again the boyish face, the feminine mouth, the sharp pointed nose.

He went out into the hall. Andrea was in the kitchen with her back to him, putting bread in the toaster. He dialled the number.

'Belfast Central.'

'May I speak to Inspector Randall, please? This is Michael Dillon calling.'

'Mr Dillon,' a new voice said. 'I'm afraid Inspector Randall isn't here. He's in Armagh today.'

'Is Chief Inspector Norton there?'

'No, he's with him, I'm afraid. If you want to leave a number I could ask Inspector Randall to ring you when he gets back.'

He gave the number at the Ormonde. 'What time do you expect him back?'

'After lunch sometime. I'll be speaking to him later on this morning. Is there a message I could give him?'

'Ask him to ring me. I have to speak to him myself.'

'OK, then. I'll give him your number.'

When he went back into the kitchen he realised that Andrea had been listening. 'When will he be back?' she asked, before he had spoken.

'After lunch.'

'Maybe you should try to get hold of the priest?'

'Stop it, will you?' he said. 'Don't nag me about it.'

'I'm not nagging you.' There was an edge of anger in her voice.

'I'm sorry. Shit, I hate doing this.'

'I know.'

But after breakfast as they walked down to the tube station she said, 'I *am* worried, you know. Will you promise me one thing? Phone me at the BBC as soon as you've spoken to him.'

'Yes, of course.'

They boarded the Northern Line tube train at Chalk Farm and changed at Tottenham Court Road, going their separate ways. In the station at the top of a long flight of elevator stairs he kissed her goodbye and watched as she went down in the morning rush. When he came out of the Underground at Green Park station and walked up Park Lane, the sky had darkened as it had the day before. Soon, it would rain.

At the entrance to the Ormonde the head doorman, recognising him, saluted. 'Morning, sir.'

'Morning.'

Harper was now on leave and as Ronny Pomfret was in a meeting with some marketing people and Helibron, the other assistant manager, had not come in yet, Dillon was nominally in charge. At once he was plunged into the familiar morning rush, checkouts, a conference with the banqueting department, a dozen minor crises which must be dealt with.

Shortly after ten when Helibron had arrived to take over, he went into the administrative offices and sat down at Harper's desk which overlooked the park. He rang the switchboard. 'This is Michael Dillon speaking. I'm taking over for John Harper for the next few weeks. If there are any personal calls for me, put them through to this desk, will you? I'm expecting a call from Northern Ireland today. Make sure I'm paged. I don't want to miss it.'

'Yes, Mr Dillon.'

At ten minutes to twelve Andrea called. He was in reception at the time and answered on a phone near the cashier's desk, so it was difficult to speak.

'Have you heard from the police?'

'Not yet.'

'Did you ring them?'

'They said he wouldn't be back until this afternoon, remember?'

'But didn't they say they would tell him you rang? Find out if they've done it.'

'I will. Now don't worry.'

'But I am worried,' she said. 'I'm worried sick.'

'I'll ring you back as soon as I speak to him. All right?'

'All right. I love you, Michael.'

'I love you, too,' he said. He saw one of the girl cashiers smile as she overheard him.

When he went into the administrative office Helibron called to him. 'What are you doing for lunch?'

He shrugged.

'Ronny's giving lunch to some Japanese. Big Hong Kong hotel group. Join us?'

'Thanks. I think I'll just have a sandwich here.'

'Well, you know where to find me. We'll be in the main restaurant.'

When Helibron had gone he sat alone in the administrative office looking out across the road at the great expanse of park. It had rained but now the sun shone and he saw groups of people lying on the grass. Joggers ran on a path parallel to the rush of traffic in Park Lane. He looked down at the traffic, the limousines, taxis and huge foreign tour buses. This was London, on a sunny summer's day. Belfast was far away. Someone came into the empty outer office. He saw that it was a bellboy bringing the afternoon newspaper and a stack of letters. The bellboy saw Dillon looking out at him and asked, 'Care for the paper, sir? *Evening Standard?*'

'No, thanks,' Dillon said, but the boy, misunderstanding, brought the paper in and gave it to him. The headline was about a murder in Brighton. He put the paper aside, but then wondered. Had anything happened?

In the newspaper there was a headline, 'N.I. POLICE SEIZE ARMS CACHE'. The dateline was *Armagh, N.I.* The story said that the police had discovered a large cache of weapons including two rocket launchers in a warehouse near Armagh. The weapons were believed to be part of a stockpile hidden by Protestant paramilitary extremists. It was suspected that the arms were part of a shipment made to the Protestant UDA from South Africa, earlier this year.

Armagh. That's why Randall and the Chief Inspector are there today. It's a big seizure. They are busy with this. The moment he was dreading, the moment he would have to tell the police that he wouldn't give evidence, would be easier today, when they were preoccupied with bigger things. Perhaps they would not come back to Belfast until tomorrow? He could not wait until tomorrow. Moira sent that priest away last night believing I will testify. The IRA will know now. They will be making plans.

Suddenly shaking, he picked up the phone and got an outside line. He dialled Randall's number.

'Belfast Central.'

'This is Michael Dillon. I'm calling Inspector Randall.'

'Mr Dillon,' a new voice said. 'Yes, we spoke this morning. He hasn't called in yet. He's in Armagh, as I told you, with Inspector Norton. I'm not sure now, if they'll be back this afternoon. But I will hear from him and I'll give him your message.'

'When you do hear from him, will you ask him if there's a number I can ring him at? It's urgent.'

'I'll do that, Mr Dillon. Not to worry. I'm sure he'll be in touch before the day's out.'

'Thank you.'

One of the secretaries came into the outer office as he put the phone down, a cheerful English girl who said, 'Have you had your lunch? I'm back now, so I'll hold the fort.'

'It's all right, I'm not hungry.'

'Your phone's blinking,' she said, sitting at her own desk and looking at the phone bank.

'Oh, sorry.' He picked it up.

'Mr Dillon. This is Helen at reception. There's someone here asking for you.'

'Who?'

'It's a Father Connolly.'

'Where is he? Is he at the desk?'

'Yes.'

'All right. I'm coming down.'

When he came out of the lift into the main lobby there were more than twenty people milling around the desk at reception. But the priest stood out from the others. He wore a shiny black straw hat, a crumpled black raincoat, and a black suit, too heavy for the London summer's sun. In his left hand he carried a cheap metal briefcase. He stood, facing the bank of lifts across the lobby and so did not see Dillon until Dillon was almost beside him.

When he did see him he turned with a small gasp, as if caught by surprise. 'Ah, there you are,' he said in his flat Belfast tones. 'Hello, Mike.'

'Hello.'

'I just got in on the shuttle. I hope I'm not taking you away from your work?'

'No, no,' Dillon said.

'Is there somewhere we could talk?'

Dillon looked past him at the main lounge. It was crowded in there. It was as though the priest were a relative he was ashamed of. He wanted to take him to a place where they would not be seen.

'Let's go over to the park,' he said. 'I could do with a breath of air.'

'Aye, it's a lovely day, right enough. It was raining when I left Belfast.'

'It usually is.'

They smiled at each other, falsely. As they went out of the hotel, Dillon said, 'How did you know where to find me?'

'I went round to the Clarence this morning and told them I was a priest and a friend of yours. They weren't keen about it at first, but finally they gave me your number here. Which, of course, they shouldn't have done. That's part of the problem.'

He did not ask what problem. They crossed Park Lane in silence and a few minutes later were in Hyde Park. 'Let's walk a while,' Dillon said.

'Right you are.'

'My wife says you spoke to her last night.'

'Ah, you've been in touch with her, then?' The priest gave him a quick, almost furtive glance. 'Then you know this lad's my nephew?'

'Yes.'

'I couldn't mention that the last time we spoke because it would have been like telling you his name. You know the police have lifted him?'

'Yes, they told me.'

Again, the priest looked at him. 'So they've been on to you already? They've asked you to come back and have a look at him, is that it?'

'Yes.'

The priest took off his straw hat and wiped his brow with the back of his hand. 'Look, there's a seat over there. Could we sit down for a minute?'

Ahead, under a large chestnut tree, was an empty park bench. They sat and the priest put his fingers inside his Roman collar, easing it as though it chafed his neck. 'Yes, he's my sister's boy. My only sister. We're very close, my sister and I. The boy's father is dead, so I've been sort of looking after them. Mike, are you sure you don't remember me from school? We were in Senior A together. Jakey McFadden's class. Dr Duffy was the head in our day.'

In the heat of a London summer's afternoon, the old classroom names were spoken like a false password, bringing back the school's draughty corridors, the musical chairs of masters rushing from class to class, priests in chalk-stained soutanes, lay masters in ragged academic gowns, the whistle and sting of the punishment cane, the crash of feet in the school chapel, the creaking silences of the study hall. Remember, remember, we were boys together. Fellow victims, word of honour, please don't tell. He looked at this stranger's red face, his anxious ice-cold eyes, his pleading smile, as he invoked that past, claiming kinship, here in a London park, to a man who did not remember him.

'Wait, wait,' the priest begged. 'There was something else about you. I remember you won the senior prize for English composition, isn't that right?'

'Look, what does it matter?'

'It matters to me, Mike. Because when my sister came to me in a terrible state, wanting help, I said to her, listen, I know him, he's a Catholic, he was in my class at St Michan's. I'll speak to him. He was at school with me. Then, when I met you, you said you didn't remember me at all. It was a real shock when you gave me that answer. When you turned me down. So when I went back and was asked what you'd said, I had to tell them the truth.'

'Tell who?'

'Kev's friends.'

'The IRA?'

'I suppose. I didn't ask.'

'You didn't need to ask, did you?' Dillon said. A sudden sense of outrage made him want to get up and walk away from this meeting.

'Listen to me, will you?' the priest said, and, irritatingly, caught hold of Dillon's arm. 'I'm trying to help you, Mike.'

'I'll bet you are.'

'What are you doing this for?' the priest asked, his fingers tight on Dillon's wrist. 'Do you really want that boy to go to jail?

What have the police ever done for you? You're a Catholic, at least you were brought up one, you know what things are like at home. The other night you and your wife were badly treated. I know that. I know you have a right to be upset about it, but listen to me, I'm telling you, your life's in danger if you go on with this. And if anything happens to you because of something I said, I'll have it on my conscience for the rest of my life. Let's not have any more killing, Mike.'

'No more killing?' Dillon wrenched his arm free of the priest's grip and stood up. 'But if I don't testify against your nephew and his friends, I'll be letting them go free to do more killing, won't I?'

'Sit down a minute, sit down. Please?' the priest said, looking around fearfully as if Dillon's remark had been overheard. 'Listen, young Kev is only nineteen. He's not a bad kid. He's had a good scare now. He's learned his lesson.'

He peered up at Dillon and when Dillon did not sit down the priest stood up, accidentally knocking over the briefcase which he had placed upright on the path beside him. 'Wait a sec,' the priest said, bending over to retrieve his case. Instead, Dillon turned and walked away, quickly in blind anger, not looking back till he reached the park railings and the exit to the street. When he did, he saw that the priest had not followed him. The priest stood, briefcase in hand, exactly where Dillon had left him, a small, lonely, insignificant figure under the huge chestnut tree.

Dillon went out of the gate and crossed Park Lane, walking back towards the hotel's elaborate entrance. Had Randall telephoned while he was out? If not, he could telephone Belfast Central now and ask them to tell Randall that he'd be over tomorrow to make the identification. Weeks or months from now, he would have to go back again for Kev's trial. He was not afraid of that. He was not afraid of them. To hell with them. He had stopped them blowing up the Clarence and killing innocent people. Now, he was going to stop them again.

He went into the lobby, and walked quickly towards the administrative office which was at the rear of the hotel. Someone called out, 'Michael?'

He turned. Andrea was running through the lobby. She ran up to him. 'Where were you? I'm so worried about you.'

'What's the matter?'

Distraught, she took hold of his arm. 'I don't know. I just had this feeling. I told them at work that I was sick and it's true. I am sick. I don't know, for some reason I have this terrible feeling. Did you call the police?'

'I did, but I haven't reached them yet. Randall and the other one, Norton, are both in Armagh. They're supposed to ring me any time now.'

'But did you leave a message? Did you say you weren't going to do it?'

'Wait,' he said. He took her hand and led her into the lounge. 'I want to talk to you. Let's sit over there, where it's quiet.'

The moment he said it, she turned to him. 'What is it, what *is* it?'

He sat her down. He told her about the priest.

'And you walked away?' she said. 'And now he's going to tell them you'll testify against his nephew?'

'Yes. I suppose so.'

'But why did you do it? You promised me. You're not going to testify, are you?'

'I feel I must. It's the right thing to do.'

'Oh, my God,' she said. 'I knew it. I had this feeling all morning. I knew something terrible was happening. He's off now, phoning them. The priest, I mean. They're not going to let you testify. They're going to kill you.'

He looked at her, at the fear in her eyes. She was trembling and on the edge of tears. 'Andrea,' he said. 'Andrea, listen. I'll have police protection.'

'What does that mean? A policeman sitting in your living-room? Following you around here in the hotel? Do you know what you're saying? Every time I open the door from now on, I'll be waiting for someone to come in and kill us.'

'Not you,' he said, but, sick, remembered that of course she was right. Wives, girlfriends, even bystanders, had been shot dead.

'And why are you doing it? It's for revenge, isn't it? Isn't that what it always is in Ireland? Revenge.'

'No.'

'Then what is it?'

'I don't know,' he said. 'I don't want to be a coward. I don't want to let them frighten me.'

'You're not a coward,' she said. 'And, if you were, is that so terrible? Is proving you're not a coward more important than our lives together? Because that's the choice you're making.'

There were tears in her eyes. She was not a coward, nor would ever be. And he, what was he? What did it matter? Why should he risk her life as well as his? Was any country worth the price that Ireland asked, a beggar's price, demanded again and again and never paid in full?

'I'm wrong,' he said, and took her hand. 'I'm sorry. It's all right. I'm not going to do it.'

She did not speak for a moment and then she said, 'I never want to go back there. Never.'

'I know.'

'You've *got* to find that priest,' she said. 'You've got to tell him.'

'He's probably on his way back to Belfast now.'

'Do you know his parish? Could you ring up and leave a message for him? He'll tell them. It would be the quickest way.'

'Look,' he said, 'I'll try the police again.'

'All right. God, I'm so worried.'

'Don't be. It's over. Come on, let's go up to my office.'

When they went into the outer room of the administrative office, the cheerful English secretary called to him. 'Oh, you're back. I thought you'd gone for the day.'

191

'This is Andrea Baxter,' he said, introducing her.

'Hello, there,' the secretary said. 'Mr Dillon, there was a call for you from an Inspector Norton.'

'When?'

'About twenty minutes ago. I told them I thought you'd be home in about an hour. They said they had your home number and that he'd ring you there.'

He looked at Andrea. 'Let's try him now,' he said. They went into Harper's office. He shut the door and dialled Randall's number. 'This is Michael Dillon. May I speak to Chief Inspector Norton, please?'

At once he was switched to a new line. 'Oh, Mr Dillon,' a voice said. 'They're not back from Armagh yet. Are you at home? Chief Inspector Norton's planning to ring you after five.'

'No, I'm not home, but I will be very shortly.'

'Good. They've arrested two more suspects in that case. The Chief Inspector is very anxious to get hold of you.'

'Thanks. I'll be at home.' He put the phone down and looked at Andrea. 'This isn't going to be easy. They've picked up two more of them. He's going to call our flat after five.'

'It's twenty to five now,' she said. 'We'd better take a cab. You don't want to miss him.'

In the taxi, going back to Hampstead, he said, 'What should I say? How am I going to put it? It's not just one they're holding now. It's three of them.'

'Just tell the truth,' she said. 'Say you're afraid. They'll know why. They must be used to it. Don't let him persuade you, that's all.'

Say you are afraid. The cab turned into Gloucester Avenue and stopped under the house sheltered by the oak tree. He got out. The driver turned the meter off. He paid the fare. The time had come. There had been no war in his life. He would never be called up as a soldier and put to the test of bravery in battle. He would never be asked to perform an act of heroism as a member of a resistance group. He had, instead, been put to the test by accident, a test he had every right to refuse. And yet as he unlatched the gate and went up to the front door of the house he knew that the moment the phone rang and he answered it, the moment he told them he was afraid, he would lose for ever something precious, something he had always taken for granted, some secret sense of his own worth.

At the front door he turned to her and said, 'Look, I'd rather be alone when I tell him. Maybe you could go and get us something for our supper? Give me half an hour.'

'I could wait in the other room. I won't listen.'

'No, please,' he said.

'All right. And, after you speak to the police, try to get hold of that priest, will you?'

'Don't worry,' he said.

She looked at him. 'Michael, you won't let him persuade you, will you?'

'No, I won't.'

She turned and went off up the avenue, going towards the shops on the high street. He unlocked the front door and went into the hall. A phone was ringing upstairs. He looked at his watch. It was just after five. He began to run upstairs, pushing past a little red-haired man who was also on his way up. 'Sorry,' he said.

'That's all right, guv.'

When he unlocked the door of the flat, the phone was still ringing. But as he went into the hall it stopped. The Chief Inspector was ringing from somewhere in Armagh. Now he would have to wait until he called back. He did not want to wait. He must get it over with now. Belfast Central must know where to reach Norton in Armagh. He went to the phone. Don't let him persuade you. Tell him the truth. You are afraid.

'Sorry, guv. Gas man.'

He turned. He had not closed the door. The little red-haired man was in the doorway. 'I've come to read the meter, sir.'

'Yes, go ahead.'

'It's in the back, here,' the meter man said, moving past him and opening the kitchen door. 'Are you Professor Robertson?' he asked, looking at a list he held in his hand.

'No, he's not here,' Dillon said. 'I'm just looking after the place for him.'

'You're Mr Dillon?'

'Yes.'

The little meter man whistled, as though calling a dog. 'Right, then,' he said.

Two young men came in at the door. They wore jeans, T-shirts, sneakers. They raised their revolvers. They were not wearing masks. This time, there would be no witness.